QUESTIONABLE SHAPES

W. D. HOWELLS

1st WORLD
LIBRARY
Literary Society

Questionable Shapes

William Dean Howells

© 1st World Library – Literary Society, 2004
PO Box 2211
Fairfield, IA 52556
www.1stworldlibrary.org
First Edition

LCCN: 2005901394

Softcover ISBN: 1-4218-1196-0
Hardcover ISBN: 1-4218-1096-4
eBook ISBN: 1-4218-1296-7

Purchase *"Questionable Shapes"*
as a traditional bound book at:
www.1stWorldLibrary.org/purchase.asp?ISBN=1-4218-1196-0

1st World Library Literary Society is a nonprofit
organization dedicated to promoting literacy by:

- Creating a free internet library accessible from any computer worldwide.
- Hosting writing competitions and offering book publishing scholarships.

Questionable Shapes
contributed by Tim, Ed & Rodney
in support of
1st World Library Literary Society

CONTENTS

HIS APPARITION.

I.

The incident was of a dignity which the supernatural has by no means always had, and which has been more than ever lacking in it since the manifestations of professional spiritualism began to vulgarize it. Hewson appreciated this as soon as he realized that he had been confronted with an apparition. He had been very little agitated at the moment, and it was not till later, when the conflict between sense and reason concerning the fact itself arose, that he was aware of any perturbation. Even then, amidst the tumult of his whirling emotions he had a sort of central calm, in which he noted the particulars of the occurrence with distinctness and precision. He had always supposed that if anything of the sort happened to him he would be greatly frightened, but he had not been at all frightened, so far as he could make out. His hair had not risen, or his cheek felt a chill; his heart had not lost or gained a beat in its pulsation; and his prime conclusion was that if the Mysteries had chosen him an agent in approaching the material world they had not made a mistake. This becomes grotesque in being put into words, but the words do not misrepresent, except by their inevitable excess, the mind in which Hewson rose, and flung open his shutters to let in the dawn upon the scene of the apparition, which he now perceived must have been, as it were, self-lighted. The robins were yelling from the trees and the sparrows bickering under them; catbirds were calling from the thickets of syringa, and in the nearest woods a hermit-thrush was ringing its crystal bells. The clear day was penetrating the east with the subtle light which precedes the sun, and a summer sweetness rose cool from the garden below, gray with dew.

In the solitude of the hour there was an intimation of privity to the event which had taken place, an implication of the unity of the natural and the supernatural, strangely different from that robust gayety of the plain day which later seemed to disown the affair, and leave the burden of proof altogether to the human witness. By this time Hewson had already set about to putting it in such phrases as should carry conviction to the hearer, and yet should convey to him no suspicion of the pride which Hewson felt in the incident as a sort of tribute to himself. He dramatized the scene at breakfast when he should describe it in plain, matter-of-fact terms, and hold every one spellbound, as he or she leaned forward over the table to listen, while he related the fact with studied unconcern for his own part in it, but with a serious regard for the integrity of the fact itself, which he had no wish to exaggerate as to its immediate meaning or remoter implications. It did not yet occur to him that it had none; they were simply to be matters of future observation in a second ordeal; for the first emotion which the incident imparted was the feeling that it would happen again, and in this return would interpret itself. Hewson was so strongly persuaded of something of the kind, that after standing for an indefinite period at the window in his pajamas, he got hardily back into bed, and waited for the repetition. He was agreeably aware of waiting without a tremor, and rather eagerly than otherwise; then he began to feel drowsy, and this at first flattered him, as a proof of his strange courage in circumstances which would have rendered sleep impossible to most men; but in another moment he started from it. If he slept every one would say he had dreamt the whole thing; and he could never himself be quite sure that he had not.

He got up, and began to dress, thinking all the time, in a dim way, how very long it would be till breakfast, and wondering what he should do till then with his appetite and his apparition. It was now only a little after four o'clock of the June morning, and nobody would be down till after eight; most people at that very movable feast, which St. John had in the English fashion, did not show themselves before nine. It was impossible to get a book and read for five hours; he would be dropping with hunger if he walked so long. Yet he must not sleep; and he must do something to keep from sleeping. He remembered a little interloping hotel, which had lately forced its way into precincts sacred to cottage life, and had impudently called itself the St. Johnswort Inn, after St. John's place, by a name which he prided himself on having poetically invented from his own and that of a prevalent wild flower. Upon the chance of getting an early cup of coffee at this hotel, Hewson finished dressing, and crept down stairs to let himself out of the house.

He not only found the door locked, as he had expected, but the key taken out; and after some misgiving he decided to lift one of the long library windows, from which he could get into the garden, closing the window after him, and so make his escape. No one was stirring outside the house any more than within; he knocked down a trellis by which a clematis was trying to climb over the window he emerged from, and found his way out of the grounds without alarming any one. He was not so successful at the hotel, where a lank boy, sweeping the long piazzas, recognized one of the St. Johnswort guests in the figure approaching the steps, and apparently had his worst fears roused for Hewson's sanity when Hewson called to him and wondered if he could get a cup of coffee at that hour; he openly owned it was an unnatural hour, and he had a fine inward sense that it was supernatural. The boy dropped his broom without a word, and vanished through the office door, reappearing after a blank interval to pick up his broom and say, "I guess so," as he began sweeping again. It was well, for one reason that he did not state his belief too confidently, Hewson thought; but after another interval of unknown length a rude, sad girl came to tell him his coffee was waiting for him. He followed her back into the still dishevelled dining room, and sat down at a long table to a cup of lukewarm drink that in color and quality recalled terrible mornings of Atlantic travel when he haplessly rose and descended to the dining-saloon of the steamer, and had a marine version of British coffee brought him by an alien table-steward.

He remembered the pock-marked nose of one alien steward, and how he had questioned whether he should give the fellow six-pence or a shilling, seeing that apart from this tribute he should have to fee his own steward for the voyage; at the same time his fancy played with the question whether that uncouth, melancholy waitress had found a moment to wash her face before hurrying to fetch his coffee. He amused himself by contrasting her sloven dejection with the brisk neatness of the service at St. Johnswort; but through all he never lost the awe, the sense of responsibility which he bore to the vision vouchsafed him, doubtless for some reason and to some end that it behooved him to divine.

WILLIAM DEAN HOWELLS

He found a yesterday's paper in the office of the hotel, and read it till he began to drowse over it, when he pulled himself up with a sharp jerk. He discovered that it was now six o'clock, and he thought if he could walk about for an hour he might return to St. Johnswort, and worry through the remaining hour till breakfast somehow. He was still framing in his thoughts some sort of statement concerning the apparition which he should make when the largest number of guests had got together at the table, with a fine question whether he should take them between the cantaloupe and the broiled chicken, or wait till they had come to the corn griddle-cakes, which St. John's cook served of a filigree perfection in homage to the good old American breakfast ideal. There would be more women, if he waited, and he should need the sympathy and countenance of women; his story would be wanting in something of its supreme effect without the electrical response of their keener nerves.

II.

When Hewson came up to the cottage he was sensible of a certain agitation in the air, which was intensified to him by the sight of St. John, in his bare, bald head and the neglige of a flannel housecoat, inspecting, with the gardener and one of the grooms, the fallen trellis under the library window, which from time to time they looked up at, as they talked. Hewson made haste to join them, through the garden gate, and to say shamefacedly enough, "Oh, I'm afraid I'm responsible for that," and he told how he must have thrown down the trellis in getting out of the window.

"Oh!" said St. John, while the two men walked away with dissatisfied grins at being foiled of their sensation. "We thought it was burglars. I'm so glad it was only you." But in spite of his profession, St. John did not give Hewson any very lively proof of his enjoyment. "Deuced uncomfortable to have had one's guests murdered in their beds. Don't say anything about it, please, Hewson. The women would all fly the premises, if there'd been even a suspicion of burglars."

"Oh, no; I won't," Hewson willingly assented; but he perceived a disappointment in St. John's tone and manner, and he suspected him, however unjustly, of having meant to give himself importance with his guests by the rumor of a burglary in the house.

　　　　　WILLIAM DEAN HOWELLS

He was a man quite capable of that, Hewson believed, and failing it, capable of pretending that he wanted the matter hushed up in the interest of others.

In any case he saw that it was not to St. John primarily, or secondarily to St. John's guests, that he could celebrate the fact of his apparition. In the presence of St. John's potential vulgarity he keenly felt his own, and he recoiled from what he had imagined doing. He even realized that he would have been working St. John an injury by betraying his house to his guests as the scene of a supernatural incident.

Nobody believes in ghosts, but there is not one in a thousand of us who would not be uncomfortable in a haunted house, or a house so reputed. If Hewson told what he had seen, he would not only scatter St. John's house-party to the four winds, but he would cast such a blight upon St. Johnswort that it would never sell for a tenth of its cost.

III.

From that instant Hewson renounced his purpose, and he remained true to this renunciation in spite of the behavior of St. John, which might well have tempted him to a revenge in kind. No one seemed to have slept late that morning; several of the ladies complained that they had not slept a wink the whole night, and two or three of the men owned to having waked early and not been able to hit it off again in a morning nap, though it appeared that they were adepts in that sort of thing. The hour of their vigils corresponded so nearly with that of Hewson's apparition that he wondered if a mystical influence from it had not penetrated the whole house. The adventitious facts were of such a nature that he controlled with the greater difficulty the wish to explode upon an audience so aptly prepared for it the prodigious incident which he was keeping in reserve; but he did not yield even when St. John carefully led up to the point through the sensation of his guests, by recounting the evidences of the supposed visit of a burglar, and then made his effect by suddenly turning upon Hewson, and saying with his broad guffaw: "And here you have the burglar in person. He has owned his crime to me, and I've let him off the penalty on condition that he tells you all about it." The humor was not too rank for the horsey people whom St. John had mainly about him, but some of the women said, "Poor Mr. Hewson!" when the host, failing Hewson's confession, went on to betray that he had risen at that unearthly hour

WILLIAM DEAN HOWELLS

to go down to the St. Johnswort Inn for a cup of its famous coffee. The coffee turned out to be the greatest kind of joke; one of the men asked Hewson if he could say on his honor that it was really any better than St. John's coffee there before them, and another professed to be in a secret more recondite than had yet been divined: it was that long grim girl, who served it; she had lured Hewson from his rest at five o'clock in the morning; and this humorist proposed a Welsh rarebit some night at the inn, where they could all see for themselves why Hewson broke out of the house and smashed a trellis before sunrise.

Hewson sat silent, not even attempting a defensive sally. In fact it was only his surface mind which was employed with what was going on; as before, his deeper thought was again absorbed with his great experience. He could not, if his conscience had otherwise suffered him, have spoken of it in that company, and the laughter died away from his silence as if it had been his offence. He was not offended, but he was ashamed, and not ashamed so much for St. John as for himself, that he could have ever imagined acquiring merit in such company by exploiting an experience which should have been sacred to him. How could he have been so shabby? He was justly punished in the humiliating contrast between being the butt of these poor wits, and the hero of an incident which, whatever its real quality was, had an august character of mystery. He had recognized this from the first instant; he had perceived that the occurrence was for him, and for him alone, until he had reasoned some probable meaning into it or from it; and yet he had been willing, he saw it, he owned it! to win the applause of that crowd as a man who had just seen a ghost.

He thought of them as that crowd, but after all, they were

good-natured people, and when they fancied that he was somehow vexed with the turn the talk had taken, they began to speak of other things; St. John himself led the way, and when he got Hewson alone after breakfast, he made him a sort of amend. "I didn't mean to annoy you, old fellow," he said, "with my story about the burglary."

"Oh, that's all right," Hewson brisked up in response, as he took the cigar St. John offered him. "I'm afraid I must have seemed rather stupid. I had got to thinking about something else, and I couldn't pull myself away from it. I wasn't annoyed at all."

Whether St. John thought this sufficient gratitude for his reparation did not appear. As Hewson did not offer to break the silence in which they went on smoking, his host made a pretext, toward the end of their cigars, after bearing the burden of the conversation apparently as long as he could, of being reminded of something by the group of women descending into the garden from the terraced walk beyond it and then slowly, with little pauses, trailing their summer draperies among the flower-beds and bushes toward the house.

"Oh, by-the-way," he said, "I should like to introduce you to Miss Hernshaw; she came last night with Mrs. Rock: that tall girl, there, lagging behind a little. She's an original."

"I noticed her at breakfast," Hewson answered, now first aware of having been struck with the strange beauty and strange behavior of the slim girl, who drooped in her chair, with her little head fallen forward, and played with her bread, ignoring her food otherwise, while she listened with a bored air to the talk which made Hewson its prey. She had an effect of being both shy and indifferent, in this

WILLIAM DEAN HOWELLS

retrospect; and when St. John put up the window, and led the way out to the women in the garden, and presented Hewson, she had still this effect. She did not smile or speak in acknowledgement of Hewson's bow; she merely looked at him with a sort of swift intensity, and then, when one of the women said, "We were coming to view the scene of your burglarious exploit, Mr. Hewson. Was that the very window?" the girl looked impatiently away.

"The very window," Hewson owned. "You wouldn't know it. St. John has had the trellis put up and the spot fresh turfed," and he detached the interlocutory widow in the direction of their bachelor host, as she perhaps intended he should, and dropped back to the side of Miss Hernshaw.

She was almost spiritually slender. In common with all of us, he had heard that shape of girl called willowy, but he made up his mind that sweetbriery would be the word for Miss Hernshaw, in whose face a virginal youth suggested the tender innocence and surprise of the flower, while the droop of her figure, at once delicate and self-reliant, arrested the fancy with a sense of the pendulous thorny spray. She looked not above sixteen in age, but as she was obviously out, in the society sense of the word, this must have been a moral effect; and Hewson was casting about in his mind for some appropriate form of thought and language to make talk in when she abruptly addressed him.

"I don't see," she said, with her face still away, "why people make fun of those poor girls who have to work in that sort of public way."

Hewson silently picked his steps back through the intervening events to the drolling at breakfast, and with some misgiving took his stand in the declaration, "You mean the waitress at the inn?"

"Yes!" cried the girl, with a gentle indignation, which was so dear to the young man that he would have given anything to believe that it veiled a measure of sympathy for himself as well as for the waitress. "We went in there last night when we arrived, for some pins - Mrs. Rock had had her dress stepped on, getting out of the car - and that girl brought them. I never saw such a sad face. And she was very nice; she had no more manners than a cow."

Miss Hernshaw added the last sentence as if it followed, and in his poor masculine pride of sequence Hewson wanted to ask if that were why she was so nice; but he obeyed a better instinct in saying, "Yes, there's a whole tragedy in it. I wonder if it's potential or actual." He somehow felt safe in being so metaphysical.

"Does it make any difference?" Miss Hernshaw demanded, whirling her face round, and fixing him with eyes of beautiful fierceness. "Tragedy is tragedy, whether you have lived it or not, isn't it? And sometimes it's all the more tragical if you have it still to live: you've got it before you! I don't see how any one can look at that girl's face and laugh at her. I should never forgive any one who did."

"Then I'm glad I didn't do any of the laughing," said Hewson, willing to relieve himself from the strain of this high mood, and yet anxious not to fall too far below it. "Perhaps I should, though, if I hadn't been the victim of it in some degree."

"It was the vulgarest thing I ever heard!" said the girl.

WILLIAM DEAN HOWELLS

Hewson looked at her, but she had averted her face again. He had a longing to tell her of his apparition which quelled every other interest in him, and, as it were, blurred his whole consciousness. She would understand, with her childlike truth, and with her unconventionality she would not find it strange that he should speak to her of such a thing for no apparent reason or no immediate cause. He walked silent at her side, revolving his longing in his thought, and hating the circumstance which forbade him to speak at once. He did not know how long he was lost in this, when he was suddenly recalled to fearful question of the fact by her saying, with another flash of her face toward him, "You *have* lost sleep Mr. Hewson!" and she whipped forward, and joined the other women, who were following the lead of St. John and the widow.

Mrs. Rock, to whom Hewson had been presented at the same time as to Miss Hernshaw, looked vaguely back at him over her shoulder, but made no attempt to include him in her group, and he thought, for no reason, that she was kept from doing so on account of Miss Hernshaw. He thought he could be no more mistaken in this than in the resentment of Miss Hernshaw, which he was aware of meriting, however unintentionally. Later, after lunch, he made sure of this fact when Mrs. Rock got him into a corner, and cozily began, "I always feel like explaining Rosalie a little," and then her vague, friendly eye wandered toward Miss Hernshaw across the room, and stopped, as if waiting for the girl to look away. But Miss Hernshaw did not look away, and that afternoon, Hewson's week being up, he left St. Johnswort before dinner.

IV.

The time came, before the following winter, when Hewson was tempted beyond his strength, and told the story of his apparition. He told it more than once, and kept himself with increasing difficulty from lying about it. He always wished to add something, to amplify the fact, to heighten the mystery of the circumstances, to divine the occult significance of the incident. In itself the incident, when stated, was rather bare and insufficient; but he held himself rigidly to the actual details, and he felt that in this at least he was offering the powers which had vouchsafed him the experience a species of atonement for breaking faith with them. It seemed like breaking faith with Miss Hernshaw, too, though this impression would have been harder to reason than the other. Both impressions began to wear off after the first tellings of the story; the wound that Hewson gave his sensibility in the very first cicatrized before the second, and at the fourth or fifth it had quite calloused over; so that he did not mind anything so much as what always seemed to him the inadequate effect of his experience with his hearers. Some listened carelessly; some nervously; some incredulously, as if he were trying to put up a job on them; some compassionately, as if he were not quite right, and ought to be looked after. There was a consensus of opinion, among those who offered any sort of comment, that he ought to give it to the Psychical Research, and at the bottom of Hewson's heart, there was a dread that the spiritualists would somehow get hold of him. This remained to stay him, when the shame of breaking faith with Miss Hernshaw and with Mystery no longer restrained him from exploiting the fact. He was aware of lying in wait for opportunities of telling it, and he swore himself to tell it only upon direct provocation, or when the occasion seemed imperatively to demand it. He commonly brought it out to match some experience of another; but he could never deny a friendly appeal when he sat with some good fellows over their five-o'clock cocktails at the club, and one of them would say in behalf of a newcomer, "Hewson, tell Wilkins that odd thing that happened to you up country, in the summer." In complying he tried to save his self-respect by affecting a contemptuous indifference in the matter, and beginning reluctantly and pooh-poohingly. He had pangs afterwards as he walked home to dress for dinner, but his self-reproach was less afflicting as time passed. His suffering from it was never so great as from the slight passed upon his apparition, when Wilkins or what other it might be, would meet the suggestion that he should tell him about it, with the hurried interposition, "Yes, I have heard that; good story." This would make Hewson think that he was beginning to tell his story too often, and that perhaps the friend who suggested his doing so, was playing upon his forgetfulness. He wondered if he were really something of a bore with it, and whether men were shying off from him at the club on account of it. He fancied that might be the reason why the circle at the five-o'clock cocktails gradually diminished as the winter passed. He continued to join it till the chance offered of squarely refusing to tell Wilkins, or whoever, about the odd thing that had happened to him up country in the summer. Then he felt that he had in a manner retrieved himself, and could retire from the five-o'clock cocktails with honor.

That it was a veridical phantom which had appeared to

him he did not in his inmost at all doubt, though in his superficial consciousness he questioned it, not indeed so disrespectfully as he pooh-poohed it to others, but still questioned it. This he thought somehow his due as a man of intelligence who ought not to suffer himself to fall into superstition even upon evidence granted to few. Superficially, however, as well as interiorly, he was aware of always expecting its repetition; and now, six months after the occurrence this expectation was as vivid with him as it was the first moment after the vision had vanished, while his tongue was yet in act to stay it with speech. He would not have been surprised at any time in walking into his room to find It there; or waking at night to confront It in the electric flash which he kindled by a touch of the button at his bedside. Rather, he was surprised that nothing of the sort happened, to confirm him in his belief that he had been all but in touch with the other life, or to give him some hint, the slightest, the dimmest, why this vision had been shown him, and then instantly broken and withdrawn. In that inmost of his where he recognized its validity, he could not deny that it had a meaning, and that it had been sent him for some good reason special to himself; though at the times when he had prefaced his story of it with terms of slighting scepticism, he had professed neither to know nor to care why the thing had happened. He always said that he had never been particularly interested in the supernatural, and then was ashamed of a lie that was false to universal human experience; but he could truthfully add that he had never in his life felt less like seeing a ghost than that morning. It was not full day, but it was perfectly light, and there the thing was, as palpable to vision as any of the men that moment confronting him with cocktails in their hands. Asked if he did not think he had dreamed it, he answered scornfully that he did not think, he *knew*, he had not dreamed it; he did not value the experience, it was and

WILLIAM DEAN HOWELLS

had always been perfectly meaningless, but he would stake his life upon its reality. Asked if it had not perhaps been the final office of a nightcap, he disdained to answer at all, though he did not openly object to the laugh which the suggestion raised.

Secretly, within his inmost, Hewson felt justly punished by the laughter. He had been unworthy of his apparition in lightly exposing it to such a chance; he had fallen below the dignity of his experience. He might never hope to fathom its meaning while he lived; but he grieved for the wrong he had done it, as if at the instant of the apparition he had offered that majestic, silent figure some grotesque indignity: thrown a pillow at it, or hailed it in tones of mocking offence. He was profoundly and exquisitely ashamed even before he ceased to tell the story for his listeners' idle amusement. When he stopped doing so, and snubbed solicitation with the curt answer that everybody had heard that story, he was retrospectively ashamed; and mixed with the expectation of seeing the vision again was the formless wish to offer it some sort of reparation, of apology.

He longed to prove himself not wholly unworthy of the advance that had been made him from the other world upon grounds which he had done his worst to prove untenable. He could not imagine what the grounds were, though he had to admit their probable existence; such an event might have no obvious or present significance, but it had not happened for nothing; it could not have happened for nothing. Hewson might not have been in what he thought any stressful need of ghostly comfort or reassurance in matters of faith. He was not inordinately agnostic, or in the way of becoming so. He was simply an average skeptical American, who denied no more than he affirmed, and who really concerned himself so little about his soul, though he tried to keep his conscience decently clean, that he had not lately asked whether other people had such a thing or not. He had not lost friends, and he was so much alone in this world that it seemed improbable the fate of any uncle or cousin, in the absence of more immediate kindred, should be mystically forecast to him. He was perfectly well at the time of the apparition, and it could not have been the figment of a disordered digestion, as the lusty hunger which willingly appeased itself with the coffee of the St. Johnswort Inn sufficiently testified. Yet, in spite of all this, an occurrence so out of the course of events must have had some message for him, and it must have been his fault that he could not divine it. A sense of culpability grew upon him with the sense of his ignominy in cheapening it by making it subservient to what he knew was, in the last analysis, a wretched vanity. At least he could refuse himself that miserable gratification hereafter, and he got back some measure of self-respect in forbidding himself the pleasure he might have taken in being noted for a strange experience he could never be got to speak of.

V.

The implication of any such study as this is that the subject of it is continuously if not exclusively occupied with the matter which is supposed to make him interesting. But of course it was not so with Hewson, who perhaps did not think of his apparition once in a fortnight, or oftener, say, than he thought of the odd girl with whom for no reason, except contemporaneity in his acquaintance, he associated with it. If he never thought of the apparition without subconsciously expecting its return, he equally expected when he thought of Miss Hernshaw that the chances of society would bring them together again, and it was with no more surprise than if the vision had intimated its second approach that he one night found her name in the minute envelope which the footman presented him at a house where he was going to dine, and realized that he was appointed to take her out. It was a house where he rather liked to go, for in that New York of his where so few houses had any distinctive character, this one had a temperament of its own in so far that you might expect to meet people of temperament there, if anywhere. They were indeed held in a social solution where many other people of no temperament at all floated largely and loosely about, but they were there, all the same, and it was worth coming on the chance of meeting them, though the indiscriminate hospitality of the hostess might let the evening pass without promoting the chance. Now, however, she had unwittingly put into Hewson's keeping, for two hours at least, the very temperament that had kept his fancy for the last half-year and more. He fairly laughed at sight of the name on the little card, and hurried into the drawing-room, where the first thing after greeting his hostess, he caught the wandering look and vague smile of Mrs. Rock. The look and the smile became personal to him, and she welcomed him with a curious resumption of the confidential terms in which they had seemed to part that afternoon at St. Johnswort. He thought that she was going to begin talking to him where she had left off, about Rosalie, as she had called her, and he was disappointed in the commonplaces that actually ensued. At the end of these, however, she did say: "Miss Hernshaw is here with me. Have you seen her?"

"Oh, yes," Hewson returned, for he had caught sight of the girl in a distant group, on his way up to Mrs. Rock, but in view of the affluent opportunity before him had richly forborne trying even to make her bow to him, though he believed she had seen him. "I am to have the happiness of going out with her."

"Oh, indeed," said Mrs. Rock, "that is nice," and then the people began assorting themselves, and the man who was appointed to take Mrs. Rock out, came and bowed Hewson away.

He hastened to that corner of the room where Miss Hernshaw was waiting, and if he had been suddenly confronted with his apparition he could not have experienced a deeper and stranger satisfaction than he felt as the girl lifted up her innocent fierce face upon him.

It brought back that whole day at St. Johnswort, of which she, with his vision, formed the supreme interest and equally the mystery; and it went warmly to his heart to have her peremptorily abolish all banalities by saying, "I was wondering if they were going to give me you, as soon as you came in."

She put her slim hand on his arm as she spoke, and he thought she must have felt him quiver at her touch. "Then you were not afraid they were going to give you me?" he bantered.

"No," she said, "I wanted to talk with you. I wanted you to tell me what Mrs. Rock said about me!"

"Just now? She said you were here."

"No, I mean that day at St. Johnswort."

Hewson laughed out for pleasure in her frankness, and then he felt a gathering up of his coat-sleeve under her nervous fingers, as if (such a thing being imaginable) she were going unwittingly to pinch him for his teasing. "She said she wanted to explain you a little."

"And then what!"

"And then nothing. She seemed to catch your eye, and she stopped."

The fingers relaxed their hold upon that gathering up of his coat-sleeve. "I won't *be* explained, and I have told her so. If I choose to act myself, and show out my real thoughts and feelings, how is it any worse than if I acted somebody else!"

"I should think it was very much better," said Hewson, inwardly warned to keep his face straight.

VI.

They had time for no more talk between the drawing-room and the dinner table, and when Miss Hernshaw's chair had been pushed in behind her, and she sat down, she turned instantly to the man on her right and began speaking to him, and left Hewson to make conversation with any one he liked or could.

He did not get on very well, not because there were not enough amusing people beside him and over against him, but because he was all the time trying to eavesdrop what was saying between Miss Hernshaw and the man on her right. It seemed to be absolute trivialities they were talking; so far as Hewson made out they got no deeper than the new play which was then commanding the public favor apparently for the reason that it was altogether surface, with no measure upwards or downwards. Upon this surface the comment of the man on Miss Hernshaw's right wandered indefatigably.

Hewson could not imagine of her sincerity a deliberate purpose of letting the poor fellow show all the shallowness that was in him, and of amusing itself with his satisfaction in turning his empty mind inside out for her inspection. She seemed, if not genuinely interested, to be paying him an unaffected attention; but when the lady across the table addressed a word to him, Miss Hernshaw, as if she had been watching for some such chance, instantly turned to Hewson.

"What do you think of 'Ghosts'?" she asked, with imperative suddenness.

"Ghosts?" he echoed.

"Or perhaps you didn't go?" she suggested, and he perceived that she meant Ibsen's tragedy. But he did not answer at once. He had had a shock, and for a timeless space he had been back in his room at St. Johnswort, with that weird figure seated at his table. It seemed to vanish again when he gave a second glance, as it had vanished before, and he drew a long sigh, and looked a little haggardly at Miss Hernshaw. "Ah, I see you did! Wasn't it tremendous? I think the girl who did Regina was simply awful, don't you?"

"I don't know," said Hewson, still so trammeled in his own involuntary associations with the word as not fully to realize the strangeness of discussing "Ghosts" with a young lady. But he pulled himself together, and nimbly making his reflection that the latitude of the stage gave room for the meeting of cultivated intelligences in regions otherwise tabooed, if they were of opposite sexes, he responded in kind. "I think that the greatest miracle of the play - and to me it was altogether miraculous" -

"Oh, I'm glad to hear you say that!" cried the girl. "It was the greatest experience of my life. I can't bear to have people undervalue it. I want to hit them. But go on!"

Hewson went on as gravely as he could in view of her potential violence: he pictured Miss Hernshaw beating down the inadequate witnesses of "Ghosts" with her fan, which lay in her lap, with her cobwebby handkerchief, drawn through its ring, and her long limp gloves looking curiously like her pretty young arms in their slenderness. "I was merely going to say that the most prodigious effect of the play was among the actors - I won't venture on the spectators - "

"No, don't! It isn't speakable."

"It's astonishing the effect a play of Ibsen's has with the actors. They can't play false. It turns the merest theatrical sticks into men and women, and it does it through the perfect honesty of the dramatist. He deals so squarely with himself that they have to deal squarely with themselves. They have to be, and not just *seem*."

Miss Hernshaw sighed deeply. "I'm glad you think that," she said, and Hewson felt very glad too that he thought that.

"Why?" he asked.

"Why? Because that is what I always want to do; and it's what I always shall do, I don't care what they say."

"But I don't know whether I understand exactly."

"Deal squarely with everybody. Say what I really feel. Then they say what they really feel."

There was an obscure resentment unworthily struggling at the bottom of Hewson's heart for her long neglect of him in behalf of the man on her left. "Yes," he said, "if they are capable of really feeling anything."

"What do you mean? Everybody really feels."

WILLIAM DEAN HOWELLS

"Well, then, thinking anything."

She drew herself up a little with an air of question. "I believe everybody really thinks, too, and it's your duty to let them find out what they're thinking, by truly saying what you think."

"Then *she* isn't dealing quite honestly with him," said Hewson, with a malicious smile.

The man at Miss Hernshaw's left was still talking about the play, and he was at that moment getting off a piece of pure parrotry about it to the lady across the table: just what everybody had been saying about it from the first.

"No, I should think she was not," said the girl, gravely. She looked hurt, as if she had been unfairly forced to the logic of her postulate, and Hewson was not altogether pleased with himself; but at least he had had his revenge in making her realize the man's vacuity.

He tried to get her back to talk about "Ghosts," again, but she answered with indifference, and just then he was arrested by something a man was saying near the head of the table.

VII.

It was rather a large dinner, but not so large that a striking phrase, launched in a momentary lull, could not fuse all the wandering attentions in a sole regard. The man who spoke was the psychologist Wanhope, and he was saying with a melancholy that mocked itself a little in his smile: "I shouldn't be particular about seeing a ghost myself. I have seen plenty of men who had seen men who had seen ghosts; but I never yet saw a man who had seen a ghost. If I had it would go a long way to persuade me of ghosts."

Hewson felt his heart thump in his throat. There was a pause, and it was as if all eyes but the eyes of the psychologist turned upon him; these rested upon the ice which the servant had just then silently slipped under them. Hewson had no reason to think that any of the people present were acquainted with his experience, but he thought it safest to take them upon the supposition that they had, and after he had said to the psychologist, "Will you allow me to present him to you?" he added, "I'm afraid every one else knows him too well already."

"You!" said his *vis-a-vis*, arching her eyebrows; and others up and down the table, looked round or over at Hewson where he sat midway of it with Miss Hernshaw drooping beside him. She alone seemed indifferent to his pretension; she seemed even insensible of it, as she broke off little corners of her ice with her fork.

WILLIAM DEAN HOWELLS

The psychologist fixed his eyes on him with scientific challenge as well as scientific interest. "Do you mean that *you* have seen a ghost?"

"Yes - ghost. Generically - provisionally. We always consider them ghosts, don't we, till they prove themselves something else? I once saw an apparition."

Several people who were near-sighted or far-placed put on their eye-glasses, to make out whether Hewson were serious; a lady who had a handsome forearm put up a lorgnette and inspected him through it; she had the air of questioning his taste, and the subtle aura of her censure penetrated to him, though she preserved a face of rigid impassivity. He returned her stare defiantly, though he was aware of not reaching her through the lenses as effectively as she reached him. Most of those who prepared themselves to listen seemed to be putting him on trial, and they apparently justified themselves in this from the cross-questioning method the psychologist necessarily took in his wish to clarify the situation.

"How long ago was it?" he asked, coldly.

"Last summer."

"Was it after dark?"

"Very much after. It was at day-break."

"Oh! You were alone?"

"Quite."

"You made sure you were not dreaming?"

"I made sure of that, instantly. I was not awakened by the apparition. I was already fully awake."

"Had your mind been running on anything of the kind?"

"Nothing could have been farther from it. I was thinking what a very long while it would be till breakfast." This was not true as to the order of the fact; but Hewson could not keep himself from saying it, and it made a laugh and created a diversion in his favor.

"How long did it seem to last?"

"The vision? That was very curious. The whole affair was quite achronic, as I may say. The figure was there and it was not there."

"It vanished suddenly?"

"I can't say it vanished at all. It ought still to be there. Have you ever returned to a place where you had always been wrong as to the points of the compass, and found yourself right up to a certain moment as you approached, and then without any apparent change, found yourself perfectly wrong again? The figure was not there, and it was there, and then it was not there."

"I think I see what you mean," said the psychologist, warily. "The evanescence was subjective."

"Altogether. But so was the apparescence."

"Ah!" said Wanhope. "You hadn't any headache?"

"Not the least."

"Ah!" The psychologist desisted with the effect of letting the defence take the witness.

A general dissatisfaction diffused itself, and Hewson felt it; but he disdained to do anything to appease it. He remained silent for that appreciable time which elapsed before his host said, almost compassionately, "Won't you tell us all about it, Mr. Hewson."

The guests, all but Miss Hernshaw, seemed to return to their impartial frame, with a leaning in Hewson's favor, such as the court-room feels when the accused is about to testify in his own behalf; the listeners cannot help wishing him well, though they may have their own opinions of his guilt.

"Why, there *isn't* any 'all-about-it,'" said Hewson. "The whole thing has been stated as to the circumstances and conditions." He could see the baffled greed in the eyes of those who were hungering for a morsel of the marvellous, and he made it as meagre as he could. He had now no temptation to exaggerate the simple fact, and he hurried it out in the fewest possible words.

VIII.

The general disappointment was evident in the moment of waiting which followed upon his almost contemptuous ending. His audience some of them took their cue from his own ironical manner, and joked; others looked as if they had been trifled with. The psychologist said, "Curious." He did not go back to his position that belief in ghosts should follow from seeing a man who had seen one; he seemed rather annoyed by the encounter. The talk took another turn and distributed itself again between contiguous persons for the brief time that elapsed before the women were to leave the men to their coffee and cigars.

When their hostess rose Hewson offered his arm to Miss Hernshaw. She had not spoken to him since he had told the story of his apparition. Now she said in an undertone so impassioned that every vibration from her voice shook his heart, "If I were you, I would never tell that story again!" and she pressed his arm with unconscious intensity, while she looked away from him.

"You don't believe it happened?" he returned.

"It did."

"Of course it happened! Why shouldn't I believe that? But that's the very reason why I wouldn't have told it. If it happened, it was something sacred - awful! Oh, I don't see how you could bear to speak of it at a dinner, when people were all torpid with - "

She stopped breathlessly, with a break in her voice that sounded just short of a sob.

"Well, I'm sufficiently ashamed of doing it, and not for the first time," he said, in sullen discontent with himself. "And I've been properly punished. You can't think how sick it makes me to realize what a detestable sensation I was seeking."

She did not heed what he was saying. "Was it that morning at St. Johnswort when you got up so early, and went for a cup of coffee at the inn?"

"Yes."

"I thought so! I could follow every instant of it; I could see just how it was. If such a thing had happened to me, I would have died before I spoke of it at such a time as this. Oh, *why* do you suppose it happened to you?" the girl grieved.

"Me, of all men?" said Hewson, with a self-contemptuous smile.

"I thought you were different," she said absently; then abruptly: "What are you standing here talking to me so long for? You must go back! All the men have gone back," and Hewson perceived that they had arrived in the drawing-room, and were conspicuously parleying in the face of a dozen interested women witnesses.

In the dining-room he took his way toward a vacant place

at the table near his host, who was saying behind his cigar to another old fellow: "I used to know her mother; she was rather original too; but nothing to this girl. I don't envy Mrs. Rock her job."

"I don't know what the pay of a chaperon is, but I suppose Hernshaw can make it worth her while, if he's like the rest out there," said the other old fellow. "I imagine he's somewhere in his millions."

The host held up one of his fingers. "Is that all? I thought more. Mines?"

"Cattle. Ah, Mr. Hewson," said the host, turning to welcome him to the chair on his other side. "Have a cigar. That was a strong story you gave us. It had a good fault, though. It was too short."

IX.

Hewson had begun now to feel a keen, persistent, painful sympathy for the apparition itself as for some one whose confidence had been abused; and this feeling was none the less, but all the more, poignant because it was he himself who was guilty towards it. He pitied it in a sort as if it had been the victim of a wrong more shocking perhaps for the want of taste in it than for any real turpitude. This was a quality of the event not without a strange consolation. In arraying him on the side of the apparition, it antagonized him with what he had done, and enabled him to renounce and disown it.

From the night of that dinner, Hewson did not again tell the story of his apparition, though the opportunities to do so now sought him as constantly as he had formerly sought them. They offered him a fresh temptation through the different perversions of the fact that had got commonly abroad, but he resisted this temptation, and let the perversions, sometimes annoyingly, sometimes amusingly, but always more and more wildly, wide of the reality, take their course. In his reticence he had the sense of atoning not only to the apparition but to Miss Hernshaw too.

Before he met her again, Miss Hernshaw had been carried off to Europe by Mrs. Rock, perhaps with the purpose of trying the veteran duplicities of that continent in breaking down the insurgent sincerity of her ward. Hewson heard that she was not to be gone a great while; it was well into the winter when they started, and he understood that they were merely going to Rome for the end of the season, and were then going to work northward, and after June in London were coming home. He did not fail to see her again before she left for any want of wishing, but he did not happen to meet her at other houses, and at the house of Mrs. Rock, if she had one, he had not been asked to call, or invited to any function. In thinking the point over it occurred to Hewson that this was so because he was not wanted there, and not wanted by Miss Hernshaw herself; for it had been in his brief experience of her that she let people know what she wanted, and that with Mrs. Rock, whose character seemed to answer to her name but poorly, she had ways of getting what she wanted. If Miss Hernshaw had wished to meet him again, he could not doubt that she would have asked him, or at the least had him asked to come and see her, and not have left it to the social fortutities to bring them together. Towards the end of the term which rumor had fixed to her stay abroad Hewson's folly was embittered to him in a way that he had never expected in his deepest shame and darkest forboding. But evil, like good, does not cease till it has fulfilled itself in every possible consequence. It seeing even more active and persistent. Good seems to satisfy itself sometimes in the direct effect, but evil winds sinuously in and out, and reaches round and over and under its wretched author, and strikes him in every tender and fatal place, with an ingenuity in finding the places out that seems truly of hell. Hewson thought he had paid the principal of his debt in full through the hurt to his vanity in failing to gain any sort of consequence from his apparition, but the interest of his debt had accumulated, and the sorest pinch was in paying the interest. His penalty took the form that was most of all distasteful to him: the form of publicity in the Sunday edition of a newspaper. A young lady attached to the staff of this journal had got hold of his story, and had made her reporter's Story of it, which she imaginatively cast in the shape of an interview with Hewson. But worse than this, and really beyond the vagary of the wildest nightmare, she gave St. Johnswort as the scene of the apparition, with all the circumstances of the supposed burglary, while tastefully disguising Hewson's identity in the figure of A Well-Known Society-man.

When Hewson read this Story (and it seemed to him that no means of bringing it to his notice at the club, and on the street, and by mail was left unemployed), he had two thoughts: one was of St. John, and one was of Miss Hernshaw. In all his exploitations of his experience he had carefully, he thought religiously, concealed the scene, except that one only time when Miss Hernshaw suddenly got it out of him by that demand of hers, "Was it that morning at St. Johnswort when you got up so early and went for a cup of coffee at the inn?" He had confided so absolutely in her that his admission had not troubled him at the time, and it had not troubled him since, till now when he found the fact given this hideous publicity, and knew that it could have become known only through her: through her who had seemed to make herself the protectress of his apparition and to guard it with indignation even against his own slight!

He could not tell himself what to think of her, and in this disability he had at least the sad comfort of literally thinking nothing of her; but he could not keep his thoughts away from St. John. It appeared to him that he thought and lived nothing else till his dread concreted itself in the letter which came from St. John as soon as that fatal newspaper could reach him, and his demand for an explanation could come back to Hewson. He wrote from St. Johnswort, where he had already gone for the season, and he assumed, as no doubt he had a right to do, that the whole thing was a fake, and that if Hewson was hesitating about denying it for fear of giving it further prominence, or out of contempt for it, he wished that he would not hesitate. There were reasons, which would suggest themselves to Hewson, why the thing, if merely and entirely a fake, should be very annoying, and he thought that it would be best to make the denial immediate and imperative. To this end he advised Hewson's sending the newspaper people a lawyer's letter; with the ulterior trouble which this would intimate they would move in the matter with a quickened conscience.

Apparently St. John was very much in earnest, and Hewson would eagerly have lied out of it, he felt in sudden depravity, from a just regard for St. John's right to privacy in his own premises, but no lying, not the boldest, not the most ingenious, could now avail. Scores of people could witness that they had heard Hewson tell the story at first hand; at second hand hundreds could still more confidently affirm its truth. But if he admitted the truth of the fact and denied merely that it had happened at St. Johnswort, he would have Miss Hernshaw to deal with and what could he hope from truth so relentless as hers? She was of a moral make so awful that if he ventured to deny it without appeal for her support (which was impossible), she was quite capable of denying his denial.

He did the only thing he could. He wrote to St. John declaring that the newspaper story, though utterly false in its pretensions to be an interview with him, was true in its essentials. The thing *had* really happened, he *had* seen an apparition, and he had seen it at St. Johnswort that

WILLIAM DEAN HOWELLS

morning when St. John supposed his house to have been invaded by burglars. He vainly turned over a thousand deprecatory expressions in his mind, with which to soften the blow but he let his letter go without including one.

X.

A week of silence passed, and then one night St. John himself appeared at Hewson's apartment. Hewson almost knew that it was his ring at the door, and in the tremulous note of his voice asking the man if he were at home, he recognized the great blubbery fellow's most plaintive mood.

"Well, Hewson," he whimpered, without staying for any form of greeting when they stood face to face, "this has been a terrible business for me. You can't imagine how it's broken me up in every direction."

"I - I'm afraid I can, St. John," Hewson began, but St. John cut him off.

"Oh, no, you can't. Look here!" He showed a handful of letters. "All from people who had promised to stay with me, taking it back, since that infernal interview of yours, or from people who hadn't answered before, saying they can't come. Of course they make all sorts of civil excuses. I shouldn't know what to do with these people if any of them came. There isn't a servant left on the place, except the gardener who lives in his own house, and the groom who sleeps in the stable. For the last three days I've had to take my meals at that infernal inn where you got your coffee."

"Is it so bad as that?" Hewson gasped.

"Yes, it is. It's so bad that sometimes I can't realize it. Do you actually mean to tell me, Hewson that you saw a ghost in my house?"

"I never said a ghost. I said an apparition. I don't know what it was. It may have been an optical delusion. I call it an apparition, because that's the shortest way out. You know I'm not a spiritualist."

"Yes, that's the devil of it," said St. John. "That's the very thing that makes people believe it *is* a ghost. There isn't one of them that don't say to himself and the other fellows that if a cool, clear-headed chap like you saw something queer, it *must* have been a ghost; and so they go on knocking my house down in price till I don't believe it would fetch fifteen hundred under the hammer to-morrow. It's simply ruin to me."

"Ruin?" Hewson echoed.

"Yes, ruin," St. John repeated. "Before this thing came out I refused twenty-five thousand for the place, because I knew I could get twenty-eight thousand. Now I couldn't get twenty-eight hundred. Couldn't you understand that the reputation of being haunted simply plays the devil with a piece of property?" "Yes; yes, I did understand that, and for that very reason I was always careful - "

"Careful! To tell people that you had seen a ghost in my house?"

"No! *Not* to tell them where I had seen a ghost. I never - "

"How did it get out then?"

"I," Hewson began, and then he stood with his mouth open, unable to close it for the articulation of the next word, which he at last huskily whispered forth, "can't tell you."

"Can't tell me?" wailed St. John. "Well, I call that pretty rough!"

"It is rough," Hewson admitted; "and Heaven knows that I would make it smooth if I could. I never once - except once only - mentioned your place in connection with the matter. I was scrupulously careful not to do so, for I did imagine something like what has happened. I would do anything - anything - in reparation. But I can't even tell you how the name of your place got out in the connection, though certainly you have a right to ask and to know. The circumstances were - peculiar. The person - was one that I wouldn't have dreamt was capable of repeating it. It was as if I had said the words over to myself."

"Well, I can't understand all that," said St. John, with rueful sulkiness, from which he brisked up to ask, as if by a sudden inspiration, "If it was only to one person, why couldn't you deny it, and throw the onus on the other fellow?" He looked up at Hewson, standing nerveless before him, from where he lay mournfully wallowing in an easy-chair, as if now for the first time, there might be a gleam of hope for them both in some such notion.

Hewson slowly shook his head. "It wouldn't work. The person - isn't that kind of person."

"Why, but see here," St. John urged. "There must be something in the fellow that you can appeal to. If you went and told him how it was playing the very deuce with me pecuniarily, he would see the necessity of letting you deny it, and taking the consequences, if he was anything of a man at all."

"He isn't anything of a man at all," said Hewson, in mechanical and melancholy parody.

"Then in Heaven's name what is he?" demanded St. John, savagely.

"A woman." "Oh!" St. John fell back in his chair. But he pulled himself up again with a sudden renewal of hope. "Why, see here! If she's the right kind of woman, she'll enjoy denying the story, and putting the people in the wrong that have circulated it!"

Hewson shook his head in rejection of the general principle, while, as to the particular instance, he could only say: "She isn't that kind. She's the kind that would rather die herself, and let everybody else die, than be party to any sort of deception."

"She must be a queer woman," St. John bewailed himself, looking at the point of his cigar, and discovering to his surprise that it was out. He did not attempt to light it. "Of course, I can't ask you *who* she is; but why shouldn't I see her, and try what *I* can do with her? I'm the one that's the principal sufferer in this matter," he added, perhaps seeing refusal in Hewson's troubled eye.

"Because - for one reason - she's in London."

"Oh Lord!" St. John lamented.

"But if she were here in New York, I couldn't allow it," he continued. "It was in confidence between us."

"She doesn't seem to have thought so," said St. John, with sarcasm which Hewson could not resent.

"There's only one thing for me to do," said Hewson, who had been thinking the point over, and saw no other way out for him as a gentleman, or even merely as a just man. He was not rich, and in the face of the mounting accumulations of other men he had grown comparatively poor, without actually losing money, since he had begun to lead the life which had long been his ideal. After carefully ascertaining at the time in question that he had sufficient income from inherited means to live without his profession, he had closed his law-office without shutting many clients out, and had contributed himself to the formation of a leisure class, which he conceived was regrettably lacking in our conditions. He had taste, he had reading, he had a pretty knowledge of the world from travel, he had observed manners, and it seemed to him that he might not immodestly pretend to supply, as far as one man went, a well-recognized want.

Hitherto he had been able to live up to his ideal with, sufficient satisfaction, and in proposing to himself never to marry, but to grow old gradually and gracefully as a bachelor of adequate income, he saw no difficulties in his way for the future, until this affair of the apparition. If now he incurred the chances of an open change in his way of living - the end was simply a question of very little time. He must not only declass, he must depatriate himself, for he would not have the means of living even much more economically than he now lived in New York, if he did what a sense of honor, of just responsibility urged him to do with regard to St. John.

He would have been glad of any interposition of Providence that would have availed him against his obvious duty. He would have liked to recall the words saying that there was only one thing for him to do, but he could not recall them and he was forced to go on. "Will you sell me your place?" he said to St. John, colorlessly.

"Sell you my place? What do you mean?"

"Simply that if you will, I shall be glad to buy it at your own valuation."

"Oh, look here, now, Hewson! I can't let you do this," St. John began, trying to feel a magnanimity which proved impossible to him. "What do you want with my place? You couldn't get anybody to live there with you."

"I couldn't afford to live there in any case," said Hewson; "but I am entirely willing to risk the purchase."

Was it possible that Hewson knew something of the neighborhood or its future, which encouraged him to take the chances of the property appreciating in value? This thought passed through St. John's mind, and he was not the man to let himself be overreached in a deal. "The place ought to be worth thirty thousand," he said, for a bluff.

It was a relief for Hewson to feel ashamed of St. John instead of himself, for a moment. "Very well, I'll give you thirty thousand."

St. John examined himself for a responsive generosity. The most he could say was, "You're doing this because of what I'd said."

"What does it matter? I make you a bonafide offer. I will give you thirty thousand dollars for St. Johnswort," said

Hewson, haughtily. "I ask you to sell me that place. I cannot see that it will ever be any good to me, but I can assure you that it would be a far worse burden for me to carry round the sense of having injured you, however unwillingly - God knows I never meant you harm! - than to shoulder the chance of your place remaining worthless on my hands."

St. John caught at the hope which the form of words suggested. "If anything can bring it up, it will be the fact that you have bought it. Such a thing would give the lie to that ridiculous story, as nothing else could. Every one will see that a house can't be very badly haunted, if the man that the ghost appeared to is willing to buy it."

"Perhaps," said Hewson sadly.

"No perhaps about it," St. John retorted, all the more cheerfully because he would have been glad before this incident to take twenty thousand for his place. "It's just on the borders of Lenox, and it's bound to come up when this blows over." He talked on for a time in an encouraging strain, while Hewson, standing with his back against the mantel, looked absently down upon him. St. John was inwardly struggling through all to say that Hewson might have the property for twenty-eight thousand, but he could not. Possibly he made himself believe that he was letting it go a great bargain at thirty; at any rate he ended by saying, "Well, it's yours - if you really mean it."

"I mean it," said Hewson.

St. John floundered up out of his chair with seal-like struggles. "Do you want the furniture?" he panted.

"The furniture? Yes, why not?" said Hewson. He did not

seem to know what he was saying, or to care.

"I will put that in for a mere nominal consideration - the rugs alone are worth the money - say a thousand more."

Hewson's man came in with a note. "The messenger is waiting, sir," he said.

Hewson was aware of wondering that he had not heard any ring. "Will you excuse me?" he said, toward St. John.

"By all means," said St. John.

Hewson opened the note, and read it with an expression which can only be described as a radiant frown. He sat down at his desk, and wrote an answer to the note, and gave it to his man, who was still waiting. Then he said to St. John, "What did you say the rugs were worth?"

"A thousand."

"I'll take them. And what do you want for the rest of the furniture?"

Clearly he had not understood that the furniture, rugs, and all, had been offered to him for a thousand dollars. But what was a man in St. John's place to do? As it was he was turning himself out of house and home for Hewson, and that was sacrifice enough. He hesitated, sighed deeply, and then said, "Well, I will throw all that in for a couple of thousand more."

"All right," said Hewson, "I will give it. Have the papers made out and I will have the money ready at once."

"Oh, there's no hurry about that, my dear fellow," said St. John, handsomely.

WILLIAM DEAN HOWELLS

XI.

Hewson's note was from Mrs. Rock, asking him to breakfast with her at the Walholland the next morning. She said that they were just off the steamer, which had got in late, and they had started so suddenly from London that she had not had time to write and have her apartment opened. She came to business in the last sentence where she said that Miss Hernshaw joined her in kind remembrances, and wished her to say that he must not fail them, or if he could not come to breakfast, to let them know at what hour during the day he would be kind enough to call; it was very important they should see him at the earliest possible moment.

Hewson instantly decided that this summons was related to the affair of his apparition, without imagining how or why, and when Miss Hernshaw met him, and almost before she could say that Mrs. Rock would be down in a moment, began with it, he made no feint of having come for anything else.

As he entered the door of Mrs. Rock's parlor, where the breakfast table was laid, the girl came swiftly toward him, with the air of having turned from watching for him at the window. "Well, what do you think of me?" she demanded as soon as she had got over Mrs. Rock's excuses for having her receive him. He had of course to repeat, "What do I think of you?" but he knew perfectly what she meant.

She disdained to help him pretend that he did not know. "It was I who told that horrible woman about your experience at St. Johnswort. I didn't dream that she was an interviewer, but that doesn't excuse me, and I am willing to take any punishment for my - I don't know what to call it - mischief."

She was so intensely ready, so magnificently prepared for the stake, if that should be her sentence, that Hewson could not help laughing. "Why there isn't any punishment severe enough for a crime like that," he began, but she would not allow him to trifle with the matter.

"Oh, I didn't think you would be so uncandid! The instant I read that interview I made Mrs. Rock get ready to come. And we started the first steamer. It seemed to me that I could not eat or sleep, till I had seen you and told you what I had done and taken the consequences. And now do you think it right to turn it off as a joke?"

"I don't wish to make a joke of it," said Hewson, gravely, in compliance with her mood. "But I don't understand, quite, how you could have got the story over there in time for you - "

"It was cabled to their London edition - that's what it said in the paper; and by this time they must have it in Australia," said Miss Hernshaw, with unrelieved severity.

"Oh!" said Hewson, giving himself time to realize that he was the psychical hero of two hemispheres. "Well," he resumed "what do you expect me to say?"

"I don't know what I expect. I expected you to say something without my prompting you. You know that it was outrageous for me to talk about your apparition without your leave, and to be the means of its getting into the newspapers."

"I'm not sure you were the means. I have told the story a hundred times, myself."

"But that doesn't excuse me. You knew the kind of people to tell it to, and I didn't."

"Oh, I am afraid I was willing to tell it to all kinds of people - to any kind that would listen."

"You are trying to evade me, Mr. Hewson," she said, with a severity he found charming. "I didn't expect that of you."

The appeal was not lost upon Hewson. "What do you want me to say?"

"I want you," said Miss Hernshaw, with an effect of giving him another trial, "to say - to acknowledge that you were terribly annoyed by that interview."

"If you will excuse me from attaching the slightest blame to you for it, I will acknowledge that I was annoyed."

Miss Hernshaw drew a deep breath as of relief. "I will arrange about the blame," she said loftily. "And now I wish to tell you how I never supposed that girl was an interviewer. We were all together at an artist's house in Rome, and after dinner, we got to telling ghost-stories, the way people do, around the fire, and I told mine - yours I mean. And before we broke up, this girl came to me - it was while we were putting on our wraps - and introduced herself, and said how much she had been impressed by my story - of course, I mean your story - and she said she supposed it was made up. I said I should not dream of making up a thing of that kind, and that it was every word true, and I had heard the person it happened to tell it himself. I don't know! I was vain of having heard it, so, at first hand."

"I can understand," said Hewson, sadly.

"And then I told her who the person was, and where it happened - and about the burglary. You can't imagine how silly people get when they begin going in that direction."

"I am afraid I can," said Hewson.

"She seemed very grateful somehow; I couldn't see why, but I didn't ask; and then I didn't think about it again till I saw it in that awful newspaper. She sent it to me herself; she was such a simpleton; she thought I would actually like to see it. She must have written it down, and sent it to the paper, and they printed it when they got ready to; she needed the money, I suppose. Then I began to wonder what you would say, when you remembered how I blamed you for telling the same story - only not half so bad - at that dinner."

"I always felt you were quite right," said Hewson. "I have always thanked you in my own mind for being so frank with me."

"Well, and what do you think now, when you know that I was ten times as bad as you - ten times as foolish and vulgar!"

"I haven't had time to formulate my ideas yet," Hewson urged.

"You know perfectly well that you despise me. Can you say that I had any right to give your name?"

"It must have got out sooner or later. I never asked any one not to mention my name when I told the story - "

"I see that you think I took a liberty, and I did. But that's nothing. That isn't the point. How I do keep beating about the bush! Mrs. Rock says it was a great deal worse to tell where it happened, for that would give the place the reputation of being haunted and nobody could ever live there afterwards, for they couldn't keep servants, even if they didn't have the creeps themselves, and it would ruin the property."

Hewson had not been able, when she touched upon this point, to elude the keen eye with which she read his silent thought.

"Is that true?" she demanded.

"Oh, no; oh, no," he began, but he could not frame in plausible terms the lies he would have uttered. He only succeeded in saying, "Those things soon blow over."

"Then how," she said, sternly, "does it happen that in every town and village, almost, there are houses that you can hardly hire anybody to live in, because people say they are haunted? No, Mr. Hewson, it's very kind of you, and I appreciate it, but you can't make me believe that it will ever blow over, about St. Johnswort. Have you heard from Mr. St. John since?"

"Yes," Hewson was obliged to own.

"And was he very much troubled about it? I should think

he was a man that would be, from the way he behaved about the burglary. Was he?" she persisted, seeing that Hewson hesitated.

"Yes, I must say he was."

There was a sound of walking to and fro in the adjoining room, a quick shutting as of trunk-lids, a noise as of a skirt shaken out, and steps advanced to the door. Miss Hernshaw ran to it and turned the key in the lock. "Not yet, Mrs. Rock," she called to the unseen presence within, and she explained to Hewson, as she faced him again, "She promised that I should have it all out with you myself, and now I'm not going to have her in here, interrupting. Well, did he write to you?"

"Yes, he wrote to me. He wanted me to deny the story."

"And did you?"

"Of course not!" said Hewson, with a note of indignation. "It was true. Besides it wouldn't have been of any use."

"No, it would have been wicked and it would have been useless. And then what did he say?"

"Nothing."

"Nothing? And you have never heard another word from him?"

"Yes, he came to see me last night."

"Here in New York? Is he here yet?"

"I suppose so."

"Where?"

"I believe at the Overpark."

Miss Hernshaw caught her breath, as if she were going to speak, but she did not say anything.

"Why do you insist upon all this, Miss Hernshaw?" he entreated. "It can do you no good to follow the matter up!"

"Do you think I want to do myself *good?*" she returned. "I want to do myself *harm!* What did he say when he came to see you?"

"Well, you can imagine," said Hewson, not able to keep out of his tone the lingering disgust he felt for St. John.

"He complained?"

"He all but shed tears," said Hewson, recalled to a humorous sense of St. John's behavior. "I felt sorry for him; though," he added, darkly, "I can't say that I do now."

Miss Hernshaw didn't seek to fathom the mystery of his closing words. "Had he been actually inconvenienced by that thing in the paper?"

"Yes - somewhat."

"How much?"

"Oh," Hewson groaned. "If you must know - "

"I must! The worst!"

"It had fairly turned him out of house and home. His servants had all left him, and he had been reduced to taking his meals at the inn. He showed me a handful of letters from people whom he had asked to visit him, withdrawing their acceptances, or making excuses for not accepting."

"Ah!" said Miss Hernshaw, with a deep, inward breath, as if this now were indeed something like the punishment she had expected. "And will it - did he think - did he say anything about the pecuniary effect - the - whether it would hurt the property?"

"He seemed to think it would," answered Hewson, reluctantly, and he added, unfortunately for his generous purpose, "I really can't enter upon that part."

She arched her eyebrows in grieved surprise. "But that is the very part that I want you to enter upon Mr. Hewson. You *must* tell me, now! Did he say that it had injured the property very much?"

"He did, but - "

"But what?"

"I think St. John is a man to put the worst face on that matter."

"You are saying that to keep me from feeling badly. But I ought to feel badly - I *wish* to feel badly. I suppose he said that it wasn't worth anything now."

"Something of that sort," Hewson helplessly admitted.

"Very well, then, I will buy it for whatever he chooses to

ask!" With the precipitation which characterized all her actions, Miss Hernshaw rose from the chair in which she had been provisionally sitting, pushed an electric button in the wall, swirled away to the other side of the room, unlocked the door behind which those sounds had subsided, and flinging it open, said, "You can come out, Mrs. Hock; I've rung for breakfast."

Mrs. Rock came smoothly forth, with her vague eyes wandering over every other object in the room, till they rested upon Hewson, directly before her. Then she gave him her hand, and asked, with a smile, as if taking him into the joke. "Well, has Rosalie had it out with you?"

"I have had it out with him, Mrs. Rock," Miss Hernshaw answered, "and I will tell you all about it later. Now I want my breakfast."

XII.

Hewson ate the meal before him, and it was a very good one, as from time to time he noted, in a daze which was as strange a confusion of the two consciousnesses as he had ever experienced. Whatever the convention was between Miss Hernshaw and Mrs. Rock with regard to the matter in hand, or lately in hand, it dropped, after a few uninterested inquiries from Mrs. Rock, who was satisfied, or seemed so, to know that Miss Hernshaw had got at the worst. She led the talk to other things, like the comparative comforts and discomforts of the line to Genoa and the line to Liverpool; and Hewson met her upon these polite topics with an apparent fulness of interest that would have deceived a much more attentive listener.

All the time he was arguing with Miss Hernshaw in his nether consciousness, pleading with her to keep her away from the fact that he had himself bought St. Johnswort, until he could frame some fitting form in which to tell her that he had bought it. With his outward eyes, he saw her drooping on the opposite side of the table, and in spite of her declaration that she wanted her breakfast, making nothing of it, after the preliminary melon, while to his inward vision she was passionately refusing, by every charming perversity, to be tempted away from the subject.

As the Cunard boats always get in on Saturday, this

morrow of their arrival was naturally Sunday; and after a while Hewson fancied symptoms of going to church in Mrs. Rock. She could not have become more vague than she ordinarily was, but her wanderings were of a kind of devotional character. She spoke of the American church in Rome, and asked Hewson if he knew the rector. Then, when he said he was afraid he was keeping her from going to church, she said she did not know whether Rosalie intended going. At the same time she rose from the table, and Hewson found that he should not be allowed to sit down again, unless by violence. He had to go away, and he went, as little at ease in his mind as he very well could be.

He was no sooner out of the house than he felt the necessity of returning. He did not know how or when Miss Hernshaw would write to St. John, but that she would do so, he did not at all doubt, and then, when the truth came out, what would she think of him? He did not think her a very wise person; she seemed to him rather a wild and whirling person in her ideals of conduct, an unbridled and undisciplined person; and yet he was aware of profoundly and tenderly respecting her as a creature of the most inexpugnable innocence and final goodness. He could not bear to have her feel that he had trifled with her. There had not been many meetings between them, but each meeting had been of such event that it had advanced their acquaintance far beyond the point that it could have reached through weeks of ordinary association. From the first there had been that sort of intimacy which exists between spirits which encounter in the region of absolute sincerity. She had never used the least of those arts which women use in concealing the candor of their natures from men unworthy of it; she had not only practiced her rule of instant and constant veracity, but had avowed it, and as it were, invited his judgment of it. Hitherto, he had met her half-way at least, but now he was in the coil of a disingenuousness which must more and more trammel him from her, unless he found some way to declare the fact to her.

This ought to have been an easy matter, but it was not easy; upon reflection it grew rather more difficult. Hewson did not see how he could avow the fact, which he wished to avow, without intolerable awkwardness; without the effect of boasting, without putting upon her a burden which he had no right to put. To be sure, she had got herself in for it all by her divine imprudence, but she had owned her error in that as promptly as if it had been the blame of some one else. Still Hewson doubted whether her magnanimity was large enough to go round in the case of a man who tried to let his magnanimity come upon her with any sort of dramatic surprise. This was what he must seem to be doing if he now left her to learn from another how he had kept St. John from loss by himself assuming the chance of depreciation in his property. But if he went and told her that he had done it, how much better for him would that be?

He took a long, unhappy walk up into the Park, and then he walked back to the Walholland. By this time he thought Mrs. Rock and Miss Hernshaw must have been to church, but he had not the courage to send up his name to them. He waited about in the region of the dining-room, in the senseless hope that it would be better for him to surprise them on their way to luncheon, and trust to some chance for introducing his confession, than to seek a direct interview with Miss Hernshaw. But they did not come to luncheon, and then Hewson had the clerk send up his card. Word came back that the ladies would see him, and he followed the messenger to Mrs. Rock's apartment, where if he was surprised, he was not disappointed to be received by Miss Hernshaw alone.

"Mrs. Rock is lying down," she explained, "but I thought that it might be something important, and you would not mind seeing me."

"Not at all," said Hewson, with what seemed to him afterwards superfluous politeness, and then they both waited until he could formulate his business, Miss Hernshaw drooping forward, and looking down in a way that he had found was most characteristic of her. "It *is* something important - at least it is important to me. Miss Hernshaw, may I ask whether you have done anything - it seems a very unwarrantable question - about St. Johnswort?"

"About buying it?"

"Yes. It will be useless to make any offer for it."

"Why will it be useless to do that?"

"Because - because I have bought it myself."

"You have bought it?"

"Yes; when he came to me last night, and made those representations - Well, in short, I have bought the place."

"To save him from losing money by that - story?"

"Well - yes. I ought to have told you the fact this morning, as soon as you said you would buy the place. I know that you like people to be perfectly truthful. But - I couldn't - without seeming to - brag."

"I understand," said Miss Hernshaw.

"I took the risk of your writing to St. John; but then I realized that if he answered and told you what I ought to have told you myself, it would make it worse, and I came back."

"I don't know whether it would have made it worse; but you have come too late," said Miss Hernshaw. "I've just written to Mr. St. John."

They were both silent for what Hewson thought a long time. At the end of it, he asked, "Did you - you must excuse me - refer to me at all?"

"No, certainly not. Why should I?"

"I don't know. I don't know that it would have mattered." He was silent again, with bowed head; when he looked up he saw tears in the girl's eyes.

"I suppose you know where this leaves me?" she said gently.

"I can't pretend that I don't," answered Hewson. "What can I do?"

"You can sell me the place for what it cost you."

"Oh, no, I can't do that," said Hewson.

"Why do you say that? It isn't as if I were poor; but even then you wouldn't have the right to refuse me if I insisted. It was my fault that it ever came out about St. Johnswort. It might have come out about you, but the harm to Mr. St. John - I did that, and why should you take it

WILLIAM DEAN HOWELLS

upon yourself?"

"Because I was really to blame from the beginning to the end. If it had not been for my pitiful wish to shine as the confidant of mystery, nothing would have been known of the affair. Even when you asked me that night if it had not happened at St. Johnswort, I know now that I had a wretched triumph in saying that it had, and I was so full of this that I did not think to caution you against repeating what I had owned."

"Yes," said the girl, with her unsparing honesty, "if you had given me any hint, I would not have told for the world. Of course I did not think - a girl wouldn't - of the effect it would have on the property."

"No, you wouldn't think of that," said Hewson. Though he agreed with her, he would have preferred that she should continue to blame herself; but he took himself severely in hand again. "So, you see, the fault was altogether mine, and if there is to be any penalty it ought to fall upon me."

"Yes," said Miss Hernshaw, "and if there has been a fault there ought to be a penalty, don't you think? It would have been no penalty for me to buy St. Johnswort. My father wouldn't have minded it." She blushed suddenly, and added, "I don't mean that - You may be so rich that - I think I had better stop."

"No, no!" said Hewson, amused, and glad of the relief. "Go on. I will tell you anything you wish to know."

"I don't wish, to know anything," said Miss Hernshaw, haughtily.

Her words seemed to put an end to an interview for which

there was no longer any excuse.

Hewson rose. "Good-by," he said, and he was rather surprised at her putting out her hand, but he took it gratefully. "Will you make my adieux to Mrs. Rock? And excuse my coming a second time to trouble you!"

"I don't see how you could have helped coming," said Miss Hernshaw, "when you thought I might write to Mr. St. John at once."

Whether this implied excuse or greater blame, Hewson had to go away with it as her final response, and he went away certainly in as great discomfort as he had come. He did not feel quite well used; it seemed to him that hard measure had been dealt him on all sides, but especially by Miss Hernshaw. After her futile effort at reparation to St. John she had apparently withdrawn from all responsibility in the matter. He did not know when he was to see her again, if ever, and he did not know what he was to wait for, if anything.

Still he had the sense of waiting for something, or for some one, and he went home to wait. There he perceived that it was for St. John, who did not keep him waiting long. His nervous ring roused Hewson half an hour after his return, and St. John came in with a look in his greedy eyes which Hewson rightly interpreted at the first glance.

"See here, Hewson," St. John said, with his habitual lack of manners. "I don't want to get you in for this thing at St. Johnswort. I know why you offered to buy the place, and though of course you are the original cause of the trouble, I don't feel that it's quite fair to let you shoulder the consequences altogether."

"Have I been complaining?" Hewson asked, dryly.

"No, and that's just it. You've behaved like a little man through it all, and I don't like to take advantage of you. If you want to rue your bargain, I'll call it off. I've had some fresh light on the matter, and I believe I can let you off without loss to myself. So that if it's me you're considering - "

"What's your fresh light?" asked Hewson.

"Well," said St. John, and he swallowed rather hard, as if it were a pill, "the fact is, I've had another offer for the place."

"A better one?"

"Well, I don't know that I can say that it is," answered St. John, saving his conscience in the form of the words.

Hewson knew that he was lying, and he had no mercy on him. "Then I believe I'll stick to my bargain. You say that the other party hasn't bettered my offer, and so I needn't withdraw on your account. I'm not bound to withdraw for any other reason."

"No, of course not." St. John rubbed his chin, as if hesitating to eat his words, however unpalatable; but in the end he seemed not to find it possible. "Well," he said, disgustedly, as he floundered up to take his leave, "I thought I ought to come and give you the chance."

"It's very nice of you," said Hewson, with a smile that made itself a derisive grin in spite of him, and a laugh of triumph when the door had closed upon St. John.

XIII.

After the first flush of Hewson's triumph had passed he
began to enjoy it less, and by-and-by he did not enjoy it at
all. He had done right not only in keeping St. John from
plundering Miss Hernshaw, but in standing firm and
taking the punishment which ought to fall upon him and
not on her. But the sense of having done right sufficed
him no more than the sense of having got the better of St.
John. What was lacking to him? In the casuistry of the
moment, which was perhaps rather emotional than
rational, it appeared to Hewson that he had again a duty
toward Miss Hernshaw, and that his feeling of
dissatisfaction was the first effect of its non-fulfilment.
But it was clearly impossible that he should go again to
see her, and tell her what had passed between him and St.
John, and it was clearly impossible that he should write
and tell her what it was quite as clearly her right to know
from him. If he went to her, or wrote to her, he felt
himself in danger of wanting to shine in the affair, as her
protector against the rapacity of St. John, and as the man
of superior quality who had outwitted a greedy fellow.
The fear that she might not admire his splendor in either
sort caused him to fall somewhat nervelessly back upon
Providence; but if the moral government of the universe
finally favored him it was not by traversing any of its own
laws. By the time he had determined to achieve both the
impossibilities which formed his dilemma - had decided
to write to Miss Hernshaw and call upon her, and leave

his letter in the event of failing to find her - his problem was as far solved as it might be, by the arrival of a note from Miss Hernshaw herself, hoping that he would come to see her on business of pressing importance.

She received him without any pretence of Mrs. Rock's intermediary presence, and put before him a letter which she had received, before writing him, from St. John, and which she could not answer without first submitting it to him. It was a sufficiently straightforward expression of his regret that he could not accept her very generous offer for St. Johnswort because the place was already sold. He had the taste to forbear any allusion to the motives which (she told Hewson) she had said prompted her offer; but then he became very darkling and sinuous in a suggestion that if Miss Hernshaw wished to have her offer known as hers to the purchaser of St. Johnswort he would be happy to notify him of it.

"You see," she eagerly commented to Hewson, "he does not give your name; but I know who it is, though I did not know when I made him my offer. I must answer his letter now, and what shall I say? Shall I tell him I know who it is? I should like to; I hate all concealments! Will it do any harm to tell him I know?"

Hewson reflected. "I don't see how it can. I was trying to come to you, when I got your note, to say that St. John had been to see me, and offered to release me from my offer, because, as I thought, you had made him a better one. He's amusingly rapacious, St. John is."

"And what did you - I beg your pardon!"

"Oh, not at all. I said I would stand to my offer."

She repressed, apparently, some form of protest, and presently asked, "And what shall I say?"

"Oh, if you like, that you have learned who the purchaser of St. Johnswort is, and that you know he will not give way."

"Well!" she said, with a quick sigh, as of disappointment. After an indefinite pause, she asked, "Shall you be going to St. Johnswort?"

"Why, I don't know," Hewson answered. "I had thought of going to Europe. But, yes, I think I shall go to St. Johnswort, first, at any rate. One can't simply turn one's back on a piece of real estate in that way," he said, recognizing a fact that would doubtless have presented itself in due order for his consideration. "My one notion was to forget it as quickly as possible."

"I should not think you would want to do that," said the girl, seriously.

"No, one oughtn't to neglect an investment."

"I don't mean that. But if such a thing had happened to me, there, I should want to go again and again."

"You mean the apparition? Did I tell you how I had always had the expectation that I should see it again, and perhaps understand it? But when I had behaved so shabbily about it, I began to feel that it would not come again."

"If I were in your place," said the girl, "I should never give up; I should spend my whole life trying to find out what it meant."

"Ah!" he sighed. "I wish you could put yourself in my place."

"I wish I could," she returned, intensely.

They looked into each other's faces.

"Miss Hernshaw," he demanded, solemnly, "do you really like people to say what they think?"

"Of course I do!"

"Then I wish you would come to St. Johnswort with me!"

"Would that do?" she asked. "If Mrs. Rock - "

He saw how far she was from taking his meaning, but he pushed on. "I don't want Mrs. Rock. I want you - you alone. Don't you understand me? I love you. I - of course it's ridiculous! We've only met three or four times in our lives, but I knew this as well the first moment as I do now. I knew it when you came walking across the garden that morning, and I haven't known it any better since, and I couldn't in a thousand years. But of course - "

"Sit down," she said, wafting herself into a chair, and he obeyed her. "I should have to tell my father," she began.

"Why, certainly," and he sprang to his feet again.

She commanded him to his chair with an imperative gesture. "I have got to find out what I think, first, myself. If I were sure that I loved you - but I don't know. I believe you are good. I believed that when they were all joking you there at breakfast, and you took it so nicely; I have *always* believed that you were good."

She seemed to be appealing to him for confirmation, but he could not very well say that she was right, and he kept silent. "I didn't like your telling that story at the dinner, and I said so; and then I went and did the same thing, or worse; so that I have nothing to say about that. And I think you have behaved very nobly to Mr. St. John." As if at some sign of protest in Hewson, she insisted, "Yes, I do! But all this doesn't prove that I love you." Again she seemed to appeal to him, and this time he thought he might answer her appeal.

"I couldn't prove that *I* love *you*, but I feel sure of it."

"And do you believe that we ought to take our feelings for a guide?"

"That's what people do," he ventured, with the glimmer of a smile in his eyes, which she was fixing so earnestly with her own.

"I am not satisfied that it is the right way," she answered. "If there is really such a thing as love there ought to be some way of finding it out besides our feelings. Don't you think it's a thing we ought to talk sensibly about?"

"Of all things in the world; though it isn't the custom."

Miss Hernshaw was silent for a moment. Then she said, "I believe I should like a little time."

"Oh, I didn't expect you to answer me at once, - I"

"But if you are going to Europe?"

"I needn't go to Europe at all. I can go to St. Johnswort, and wait for your answer there."

"It might be a good while," she urged. "I should want to tell my father that I was thinking about it, and he would want to see you before he approved."

"Why, of course!"

"Not," she added, "that it would make any difference, if I was sure of it myself. He has always said that he would not try to control me in such a matter, and I think he would like you. I do like you very much myself, Mr. Hewson, but I don't think it would be right to say I loved you unless I could prove it."

Hewson was tempted to say that she could prove it by marrying him, but he had not the heart to mock a scruple which he felt to be sacred. What he did say was: "Then I will wait till you can prove it. Do you wish me not to see you again, before you have made up your mind?"

"I don't know. I can't see what harm there would be in our meeting." "No, I can't, either," said Hewson, as she seemed to refer the point to him. "Should you mind my coming again, say, this evening?"

"To-night?" She reflected a moment. "Yes, come to-night."

When he came after dinner, Hewson was sensible from the perfectm unconsciousness of Mrs. Rock's manner that Miss Hernshaw had been telling her. Her habit of a wandering eye, contributed to the effect she wished to produce, if this were the effect, and her success was such that it might easily have deceived herself. But when Mrs. Rock, in a supreme exercise of her unconsciousness, left him with the girl for a brief interval before it was time for him to go, Miss Hernshaw said, "Mrs. Rock knows about it, and she says that the best way for me to find out will be to try whether I can live without you."

"Was that Mrs. Rock's idea?" asked Hewson, as gravely as he could.

"No it was mine; I suggested it to her; but she approves of it. Don't you like it?"

"Yes. I hope I sha'n't die while you are trying to live without me. Shall you be very long?" She frowned, and he hastened to say, "I do like your idea; it's the best way, and I thank you for giving me a chance."

"We are going out to my father's ranch in Colorado, at once," she explained. "We shall start to-morrow morning."

"Oh! May I come to see you off?"

"No, I would rather begin at once."

"May I write to you?"

"I will write to you - when I've decided."

She gave him her hand, but she would not allow him to keep it for more than farewell, and then she made him stay till Mrs. Rock came back, and take leave of her too; he had frankly forgotten Mrs. Rock, who bade him adieu with averted eyes, and many civilities about seeing him again. She could hardly have been said to be seeing him then.

XIV.

The difficulties of domestication at St. Johnswort had not been misrepresented by the late proprietor, Hewson found, when he went to take possession of his estate. He thought it right in engaging servants to say openly that the place had the reputation of being haunted, and if he had not thought it right he would have thought it expedient, for he knew that if he had concealed the fact it would have been discovered to them within twenty-four hours of their arrival. His declaration was sufficient at once with most, who recoiled from his service as if he had himself been a ghost; with one or two sceptics who seemed willing to take the risks (probably in a guilty consciousness of records that would have kept them out of other employ) his confession that he had himself seen the spectre which haunted St. Johnswort, was equally effective. He prevailed at last against the fact and his own testimony with a Japanese, who could not be made to understand the objection to the place, and who willingly went with Hewson as his valet and general house-workman. With the wife of the gardener coming in to cook for them during the long daylight, he got on in as much comfort as he could have expected, and by night he suffered no sort of disturbance from the apparition. He had expected to be annoyed by believers in spiritualism, and other psychical inquirers, but it sufficed with them to learn from him that he had come to regard his experience, of which he had no more question now than ever, as purely subjective.

It seemed to Hewson, in the six weeks' time which he spent at St. Johnswort, waiting to hear from Rosalie (he had come already to think of her as Rosalie), that all his life was subjective, it passed so like a dream. He had some outward cares as to the place; he kept a horse in the stable, where St. John had kept half a dozen, and he had the gardener look after that as well as the shrubs and vegetables; but all went on in a suspensive and provisional sort. In the mean time Rosalie's charm grew upon him; everything that she had said or looked, was hourly and daily sweeter and dearer; her truth was intoxicating, beyond the lures of other women, in which the quality of deceit had once fascinated him. Now, so late in his youthful life, he realized that there was no beauty but that of truth, and he pledged himself a thousand times that if she should say she could not live without him he would henceforward live for truth alone, and not for the truth merely as it was in her, but as it was in everything. In those day's he learned to know himself, as he never had before, and to put off a certain shell of worldliness that had grown upon him. In his remoteness from it, New York became very distasteful to him; he thought with reluctance of going back to it; his club, which had been his home, now appeared a joyless exile; the life of a leisure class, which he had made his ideal, looked pitifully mean and little in the retrospect; he wondered how he could have valued the things that he had once thought worthy. He did not know what he should replace it all with, but Rosalie would know, in the event of not being able to live without him. In that event there was hardly any use of which he could not be capable. In any other event - he surprised himself by realizing that in any other event - still the universe had somehow more meaning than it once had. Somehow, he felt himself an emancipated man.

He began many letters to Rosalie, and some he finished and some not, but he sent none; and when her letter came at last, he was glad that he had waited for it in implicit trust of its coming, though he believed she would have forgiven him if he had not had the patience. The letter was quite what he could have imagined of her. She said that she had put herself thoroughly to the test, and she could not live without him. But if he had found out that he could live without her, then she should know that she had been to blame, and would take her punishment. Apparently in her philosophy, which now seemed to him so divine, without punishment there must be perdition; it was the penalty that redeemed; that was the token of forgiveness.

Hewson hurried out to Colorado, where he found Hernshaw a stout, silent, impersonal man, whose notion of the paternal office seemed to be a ready acquiescence in a daughter's choice of a husband; he appeared to think this could be best expressed to Hewson in a good cigar He perceptibly enjoyed the business details of the affair, but he enjoyed despatching them in the least possible time and the fewest words, and then he settled down to the pleasure of a superficial passivity. Hewson could not make out that he regarded his daughter as at all an unusual girl, and from this he argued that her mother must have been a very unusual woman. His only reason for doubting that Rosalie must have got all her originality from her mother was something that fell from Hernshaw when they were near the end of their cigars. He said irrelevantly to their talk at that point, "I suppose you know Rosalie believes in that ghost of yours?"

"Was it a ghost? - I've never been sure, myself," said Hewson.

"How do you explain it?" asked his prospective father-in-law.

"I don't explain it. I have always left it just as it was. I know that it was a real experience."

"I think I should have left it so, too," said Hernshaw. "That always gives it a chance to explain itself. If such a thing had happened to me I should give it all the time it wanted."

"Well, I haven't hurried it," Hewson suggested.

"What I mean," and Hernshaw stepped to the edge of the porch and threw the butt of his cigar into the darkness, where it described a glimmering arc, "is that if anything came to me that would help shore up my professed faith in what most of us want to believe in, I would take the common-law view of it. I would believe it was innocent till it proved itself guilty. I wouldn't try to make it out a fraud myself."

"I'm afraid that's what I've really done," said Hewson. "But before people I've put up a bluff of despising it." "Oh, yes, I understand that," said Hernshaw. "A man thinks that if he can have an experience like that he must be something out of the common, and if he can despise it - "

"You've hit my case exactly," said Hewson, and the two men laughed.

XV.

After his marriage, which took place without needless delay, Hewson returned with his wife to spend their honey-moon at St. Johnswort. The honey-moon prolonged itself during an entire year, and in this time they contrived so far to live down its reputation of being a haunted house that they were able to conduct their *menage* on the ordinary terms. They themselves never wished to lose the sense of something supernatural in the place, and were never quite able to accept the actual conditions as final. That is to say, Rosalie was not, for she had taken Hewson's apparition under her peculiar care, and defended it against even his question. She had a feeling (it was scarcely a conviction) that if he believed more strenuously in the validity of his apparition as an authorized messenger from the unseen world it would yet come again and declare its errand. She could not accept the theory that if such a thing actually happened it could happen for nothing at all, or that the reason of its occurrence could be indefinitely postponed. She was impatient of that, as often as he urged the possibility, and she wished him to use a seriousness of mind in speaking of his apparition which should form some sort of atonement to it for his past levity, though since she had taken his apparition into her keeping he had scarcely hazarded any suggestion concerning it; in fact it had become so much her apparition that he had a fantastic reluctance from meddling with it.

"You are always requiring a great occasion for it," he said, at last. "What greater event could it have foreshadowed or foreshown, than that which actually came to pass?"

"I don't understand you, Arthur," she said, letting her hand creep into his, where it trembled provisionally as they sat together in the twilight.

"Why, that was the day I first saw you."

"Now, you are laughing!" she said, pulling her hand away.

"Indeed, I'm not! I couldn't imagine anything more important than the union of our lives. And if that was what the apparition meant to portend it could not have intimated it by a more noble and impressive behavior. Simply to be there, and then to be gone, and leave the rest to us! It was majestic, it was - delicate!"

"Yes, it was. But it was too much, for it was out of proportion. A mere earthly love-affair - " "Is it merely for earth?"

"Oh, husband, I hope you don't think so! I wanted you to say you didn't. And if you don't think so, yes, I'll believe it came for that!"

"You may be sure I don't think so."

"Then I know it will come again."

THE ANGEL OF THE LORD.

I.

"All that sort of personification," said Wanhope, "is far less remarkable than the depersonification which has now taken place so thoroughly that we no longer think in the old terms at all. It was natural that the primitive peoples should figure the passions, conditions, virtues, vices, forces, qualities, in some sort of corporal shape, with each a propensity or impulse of its own, but it does not seem to me so natural that the derivative peoples should cease to do so. It is rational that they should do so, and I don't know that any stronger proof of our intellectual advance could be alleged than the fact that the old personifications survive in the parlance while they are quite extinct in the consciousness. We still talk of death at times as if it were an embodied force of some kind, and of love in the same way; but I don't believe that any man of the commonest common-school education thinks of them so. If you try to do it yourself, you are rather ashamed of the puerility, and when a painter or a sculptor puts them in an objective shape, you follow him with impatience, almost with contempt."

"How about the poets?" asked Minver, less with the notion, perhaps, of refuting the psychologist than of bringing the literary member of our little group under the disgrace that had fallen upon him as an artist.

"The poets," said I, "are as extinct as the personifications."

"That's very handsome of you, Acton," said the artist. "But go on, Wanhope."

"Yes, get down to business," said Rulledge. Being of no employ whatever, and spending his whole life at the club in an extraordinary idleness, Rulledge was always using the most strenuous expressions, and requiring everybody to be practical. He leaned directly forward with the difficulty that a man of his girth has in such a movement, and vigorously broke off the ash of his cigar against the edge of his saucer. We had been dining together, and had been served with coffee in the Turkish room, as it was called from its cushions and hangings of Indian and Egyptian stuffs. "What is the instance you've got up your sleeve?" He smoked with great energy, and cast his eyes alertly about as if to make sure that there was no chance of Wanhope's physically escaping him, from the corner of the divan, where he sat pretty well hemmed in by the rest of us, spreading in an irregular circle before him.

"You unscientific people are always wanting an instance, as if an instance were convincing. An instance is only suggestive; a thousand instances, if you please, are convincing," said the psychologist. "But I don't know that I wish to be convincing. I would rather be enquiring. That is much more interesting, and, perhaps, profitable."

"All the same," Minver persisted, apparently in behalf of Rulledge, but with an after-grudge of his own, "you'll allow that you were thinking of something in particular when you began with that generalization about the lost art of personifying?"

"Oh, that is very curious," said the psychologist. "We talk of generalizing, but is there any such thing? Aren't we always striving from one concrete to another, and isn't what we call generalizing merely a process of finding our way?"

"I see what you mean," said the artist, expressing in that familiar formula the state of the man who hopes to know what the other man means.

"That's what I say," Rulledge put in. "You've got something up your sleeve. What is it?"

Wanhope struck the little bell on the table before him, but, without waiting for a response, he intercepted a waiter who was passing with a coffee-pot, and asked, "Oh, couldn't you give me some of that?"

The man filled his cup for him, and after Wanhope put in the sugar and lifted it to his lips, Rulledge said, with his impetuous business air, "It's easy to see what Wanhope does his high thinking on."

"Yes," the psychologist admitted, "coffee is an inspiration. But you can overdo an inspiration. It would be interesting to know whether there hasn't been a change in the quality of thought since the use of such stimulants came in - whether it hasn't been subtilized - "

"Was that what you were going to say?" demanded Rulledge, relentlessly. "Come, we've got no time to throw away!"

Everybody laughed.

"*You* haven't, anyway," said I.

"Well, none of his own," Minver admitted for the idler.

"I suppose you mean I have thrown it all away. Well, I don't want to throw away other peoples'. Go on, Wanhope."

II.

The psychologist set his cup down and resumed his cigar, which he had to pull at pretty strongly before it revived. "I should not be surprised," he began, "if a good deal of the fear of death had arisen, and perpetuated itself in the race, from the early personification of dissolution as an enemy of a certain dreadful aspect, armed and threatening. That conception wouldn't have been found in men's minds at first; it would have been the result of later crude meditation upon the fact. But it would have remained through all the imaginative ages, and the notion might have been intensified in the more delicate temperaments as time went on, and by the play of heredity it might come down to our own day in certain instances with a force scarcely impaired by the lapse of incalculable time."

"You said just now," said Rulledge, in rueful reproach, "that personification had gone out."

"Yes, it has. I did say that, and yet I suppose that though such a notion of death, say, no longer survives in the consciousness, it does survive in the unconsciousness, and that any vivid accident or illusory suggestion would have force to bring it to the surface."

"I wish I knew what you were driving at," said Rulledge.

"You remember Ormond, don't you?" asked Wanhope,

turning suddenly to me.

"Perfectly," I said. "I - he isn't living, is he?"

"No; he died two years ago."

"I thought so," I said, with the relief that one feels in not having put a fellow-creature out of life, even conditionally.

"You knew Mrs. Ormond, too, I believe," the psychologist pursued.

I owned that I used to go to the Ormonds' house.

"Then you know what a type she was, I suppose," he turned to the others, "and as they're both dead it's no contravention of the club etiquette against talking of women, to speak of her. I can't very well give the instance - the sign - that Rulledge is seeking without speaking of her, unless I use a great deal of circumlocution." We all urged him to go on, and he went on. "I had the facts I'm going to give, from Mrs. Ormond. You know that the Ormonds left New York a couple of years ago?"

He happened to look at Minver as he spoke, and Minver answered: "No; I must confess that I didn't even know they had left the planet."

Wanhope ignored his irrelevant ignorance. "They went to live provisionally at a place up the Housatonic road, somewhere - perhaps Canaan; but it doesn't matter. Ormond had been suffering some time with an obscure affection of the heart - "

"Oh, come now!" said Rulledge. "You're not going to

spring anything so pat as heart-disease on us?"

"Acton is all ears," said Minver, nodding toward me. "He hears the weird note afar."

The psychologist smiled. "I'm afraid you're not interested. I'm not much interested myself in these unrelated instances."

"Oh, no!" "Don't!" "Do go on!" the different entreaties came, and after a little time taken to recover his lost equanimity, Wanhope went on: "I don't know whether you knew that Ormond had rather a peculiar dread of death." We none of us could affirm that we did, and again Wanhope resumed: "I shouldn't say that he was a coward above other men I believe he was rather below the average in cowardice. But the thought of death weighed upon him. You find this much more commonly among the Russians, if we are to believe their novelists, than among Americans. He might have been a character out of one of Tourguenief's books, the idea of death was so constantly present with him. He once told me that the fear of it was a part of his earliest consciousness, before the time when he could have had any intellectual conception of it. It seemed to be something like the projection of an alien horror into his life - a prenatal influence - "

"Jove!" Rulledge broke in. "I don't see how the women stand it. To look forward nearly a whole year to death as the possible end of all they're hoping for and suffering for! Talk of men's courage after that! I wonder we're not *all* marked.'

"I never heard of anything of the kind in Ormond's history," said Wanhope, tolerant of the incursion.

Minver took his cigar out to ask, the more impressively, perhaps, "What do you fellows make of the terror that a two months' babe starts in its sleep with before it can have any notion of what fear is on its own hook?"

"We don't make anything of it," the psychologist answered. "Perhaps the pathologists do."

"Oh, it's easy enough to say wind," Rulledge indignantly protested.

"Too easy, I agree with you," Wanhope consented. "We cannot tell what influences reach us from our environment, or what our environment really is, or how much or little we mean by the word. The sense of danger seems to be inborn, and possibly it is a survival of our race life when it was wholly animal and took care of itself through what we used to call the instincts. But, as I was saying, it was not danger that Ormond seemed to be afraid of, if it came short of death. He was almost abnormally indifferent to pain. I knew of his undergoing an operation that most people would take ether for, and not wincing, because it was not supposed to involve a fatal result.

"Perhaps he carried his own anodyne with him," said Minver, "like the Chinese."

"You mean a sort of self-anaesthesia?" Wanhope asked. "That is very interesting. How far such a principle, if there is one, can be carried in practice. The hypnotists - "

"I'm afraid I didn't mean anything so serious or scientific," said the painter.

"Then don't switch Wanhope off on a side track," Rulledge implored. "You know how hard it is to keep him on the main line. He's got a mind that splays all over the place if you give him the least chance. Now, Wanhope, come down to business."

Wanhope laughed amiably. "Why, there's so very little of the business. I'm not sure that it wasn't Mrs. Ormond's attitude toward the fact that interested me most. It was nothing short of devout. She was a convert. She believed he really saw - I suppose," he turned to me, "there's no harm in our recognizing now that they didn't always get on smoothly together?"

"Did they ever?" I asked.

"Oh, yes - oh, yes," said the psychologist, kindly. "They were very fond of each other, and often very peaceful."

"I never happened to be by," I said.

"Used to fight like cats and dogs," said Minver. "And they didn't seem to mind people. It was very swell, in a way, their indifference, and it did help to take away a fellow's embarrassment."

"That seemed to come mostly to an end that summer," said Wanhope, "if you could believe Mrs. Ormond."

"You probably couldn't," the painter put in.

"At any rate she seemed to worship his memory."

"Oh, yes; she hadn't him there to claw."

"Well, she was quite frank about it with me," the psychologist pursued. "She admitted that they had always quarreled a good deal. She seemed to think it was a token of their perfect unity. It was as if they were each quarreling with themselves, she said. I'm not sure that there wasn't something in the notion. There is no doubt but that they were tremendously in love with each other, and there is something curious in the bickerings of married people if they are in love. It's one way of having no concealments; it's perfect confidence of a kind - "

"Or unkind," Minver suggested.

"What has all that got to do with it!" Rulledge demanded.

"Nothing directly," Wanhope confessed, "and I'm not sure that it has much to do indirectly. Still, it has a certain atmospheric relation. It is very remarkable how thoughts connect themselves with one another. It's a sort of wireless telegraphy. They do not touch at all; there is apparently no manner of tie between them, but they communicate - "

"Oh, Lord!" Rulledge fumed.

Wanhope looked at him with a smiling concern, such as a physician might feel in the symptoms of a peculiar case. "I wonder," he said absently, "how much of our impatience with a fact delayed is a survival of the childhood of the race, and how far it is the effect of conditions in which possession is the ideal!"

Rulledge pushed back his chair, and walked away in dudgeon. "I'm a busy man myself. When you've got anything to say you can send for me."

Minver ran after him, as no doubt he meant some one should. "Oh, come back! He's just going to begin;" and

WILLIAM DEAN HOWELLS

when Rulledge, after some pouting, had been *pushed down into his chair again,* Wanhope went on, with a glance of scientific pleasure at him.

III.

"The house they had taken was rather a lonely place, out of sight of neighbors, which they had got cheap because it was so isolated and inconvenient, I fancy. Of course Mrs. Ormond, with her exaggeration, represented it as a sort of solitude which nobody but tramps of the most dangerous description ever visited. As she said, she never went to sleep without expecting to wake up murdered in her bed."

"Like her," said Minver, with a glance at me full of relish for the touch of character which I would feel with him.

"She said," Wanhope went on, "that she was anxious from the first for the effect upon Ormond. In the stress of any danger, she gave me to understand, he always behaved very well, but out of its immediate presence he was full of all sorts of gloomy apprehensions, unless the surroundings were cheerful. She could not imagine how he came to take the place, but when she told him so - "

"I've no doubt she told him so pretty promptly," the painter grinned.

"- he explained that he had seen it on a brilliant day in spring, when all the trees were in bloom, and the bees humming in the blossoms, and the orioles singing, and the outlook from the lawn down over the river valley was at its best. He had fallen in love with the place, that was the

WILLIAM DEAN HOWELLS

truth, and he was so wildly in love with it all through that he could not feel the defect she did in it. He used to go gaily about the wide, harking old house at night, shutting it up, and singing or whistling while she sat quaking at the notion of their loneliness and their absolute helplessness - an invalid and a little woman - in case anything happened. She wanted him to get the man who did the odd jobs about the house, to sleep there, but he laughed at her, and they kept on with their usual town equipment of two serving-women. She could not account for his spirits, which were usually so low when they were alone - "

"And not fighting," Minver suggested to me.

"- and when she asked him what the matter was he could not account for them, either. But he said, one day, that the fear of death seemed to be lifted from his soul, and that made her shudder."

Rulledge fetched a long sigh, and Minver interpreted, "Beginning to feel that it's something like now."

"He said that for the first time within his memory he was rid of that nether consciousness of mortality which had haunted his whole life, and poisoned, more or less, all his pleasure in living. He had got a reprieve, or a respite, and he felt like a boy - another kind of boy from what he had ever been. He was full of all sorts of brilliant hopes and plans. He had visions of success in business beyond anything he had known, and talked of buying the place he had taken, and getting a summer colony of friends about them. He meant to cut the property up, and make the right kind of people inducements. His world seemed to have been emptied of all trouble as well as all mortal danger."

"Haven't you psychologists some message about a

condition like that!" I asked.

"Perhaps it's only the pathologists again," said Minver.

"The alienists, rather more specifically," said Wanhope. "They recognize it as one of the beginnings of insanit - *folie des grandeurs* as the French call the stage."

"Is it necessarily that?" Rulledge demanded, with a resentment which we felt so droll in him that we laughed.

"I don't know that it is," said Wanhope. "I don't know why we shouldn't sometimes, in the absence of proofs to the contrary, give such a fact the chance to evince a spiritual import. Of course it had no other import to poor Mrs. Ormond, and of course I didn't dream of suggesting a scientific significance."

"I should think not!" Rulledge puffed.

Wanhope went on: "I don't think I should have dared to do so to a woman in her exaltation concerning it. I could see that however his state had affected her with dread or discomfort in the first place, it had since come to be her supreme hope and consolation. In view of what afterward happened, she regarded it as the effect of a mystical intimation from another world that was sacred, and could not he considered like an ordinary fact without sacrilege. There was something very pathetic in her absolute conviction that Ormond's happiness was an emanation from the source of all happiness, such as sometimes, where the consciousness persists, comes to a death-bed. That the dying are not afraid of dying is a fact of such common, such almost invariable observation - "

"You mean," I interposed, "when the vital forces are

WILLIAM DEAN HOWELLS

beaten so low that the natural dread of ceasing to be, has no play? It has less play, I've noticed, in age than in youth, but for the same reason that it has when people are weakened by sickness."

"Ah," said Wanhope, "that comparative indifference to death in the old, to whom it is so much nearer than it is to the young, is very suggestive. There may be something in what you say; they may not care so much because they have no longer the strength - the muscular strength - for caring. They are too tired to care as they used. There is a whole region of most important inquiry in that direction - "

"Did you mean to have him take that direction?" Rulledge asked, sulkily.

"He can take any direction for me," I said. "He is always delightful."

"Ah, thank you!" said Wanhope.

"But I confess," I went on, "that I was wondering whether the fact that the dying are indifferent to death could be established in the case of those who die in the flush of health and strength, like, for instance, people who are put to death."

Wanhope smiled. "I think it can - measurably. Most murderers make a good end, as the saying used to be, when they end on the scaffold, though they are not supported by religious fervor of any kind, or the exaltation of a high ideal. They go meekly and even cheerfully to their death, without rebellion or even objection. It is most exceptional that they make a fight for their lives, as that woman did a few years ago at

Dannemora, and disgusted all refined people with capital punishment."

"I wish they would make a fight always," said Rulledge, with unexpected feeling. "It would do more than anything to put an end to that barbarity."

"It would be very interesting, as Wanhope says," Minver remarked. "But aren't we getting rather far away? From the Ormonds, I mean."

"We are, rather," said Wanhope. "Though I agree that it would be interesting. I should rather like to have it tried. You know Frederick Douglass acted upon some such principle when his master attempted to whip him. He fought, and he had a theory that if the slave had always fought there would soon have been an end of whipping, and so an end of slavery. But probably it will be a good while before criminals are - "

"Educated up to the idea," Minver proposed.

"Yes," Wanhope absently acquiesced. "There seems to be a resignation intimated to the parting soul, whether in sickness or in health, by the mere proximity of death. In Ormond's case there seems to have been something more positive. His wife says that in the beginning of those days he used to come to her and wonder what could be the matter with him. He had a joy he could not account for by anything in their lives, and it made her tremble."

"Probably it didn't. I don't think there was anything that could make Mrs. Ormond tremble, unless it was the chance that Ormond would get the last word," said Minver.

No one minded him, and Wanhope continued: "Of course she thought he must be going to have a fit of sickness, as the people say in the country, or used to say. Those expressions often survive in the common parlance long after the peculiar mental and moral conditions in which they originated have passed away. They must once have been more accurate than they are now. When one said 'fit of sickness' one must have meant something specific; it would be interesting to know what. Women use those expressions longer than men; they seem to be inveterate in their nerves; and women apparently do their thinking in their nerves rather than their brains."

IV.

Wanhope had that distant look in his eyes which warned his familiars of a possible excursion, and I said, in the hope of keeping him from it, "Then isn't there a turn of phrase somewhat analogous to that in a personification?"

"Ah, yes - a personification," he repeated with a freshness of interest, which he presently accounted for. "The place they had taken was very completely furnished. They got it fully equipped, even to linen and silver; but what was more important to poor Ormond was the library, very rich in the English classics, which appeared to go with the house. The owner was a girl who married and lived abroad, and these were her father's books. Mrs. Ormond said that her husband had the greatest pleasure in them: their print, which was good and black, and their paper, which was thin and yellowish, and their binding, which was tree calf in the poets, he specially liked. They were English editions as well as English classics, and she said he caressed the books, as he read them, with that touch which the book-lover has; he put his face into them, and inhaled their odor as if it were the bouquet of wine; he wanted her to like it, too."

"Then she hated it," Minver said, unrelentingly.

"Perhaps not, if there was nobody else there," I urged.

For once Wanhope was not to be tempted off on another scent. "There was a good deal of old-fashioned fiction of the suspiratory and exclamatory sort, like Mackenzie's, and Sterne's and his followers, full of feeling, as people understood feeling a hundred years ago. But what Ormond rejoiced in most were the poets, good and bad, like Gray and Collins and Young, and their contemporaries, who personified nearly everything from Contemplation to Indigestion, through the whole range of the Vices, Virtues, Passions, Propensities, Attributes, and Qualities, and gave them each a dignified capital letter to wear. She said he used to come roaring to her with the passages in which these personifications flourished, and read them off with mock admiration, and then shriek and sputter with laughter. You know the way he had when a thing pleased him, especially a thing that had some relish of the quaint or rococo. As nearly as she would admit, in view of his loss, he bored her with these things. He was always hunting down some new personification, and when he had got it, adding it to the list he kept. She said he had thousands of them, but I suppose he had not so many. He had enough, though, to keep him amused, and she said he talked of writing something for the magazines about them, but probably he never would have done it. He never wrote anything, did he?" Wanhope asked of me.

"Oh, no. He was far too literary for *that*," I answered. "He had a reputation to lose."

"Pretty good," said Minver, "even if Ormond *is* dead."

Wanhope ignored us both. "After awhile, his wife said, she began to notice a certain change in his attitude toward the personifications. She noticed this, always expecting that fit of sickness for him; but she was not so much troubled by his returning seriousness. Oh, I ought to tell you that when she first began to be anxious for him she privately wrote home to their family doctor, telling him how strangely happy Ormond was, and asking him if he could advise anything. He wrote back that if Ormond was so very happy they had better not do anything to cure him; that the disease was not infectious, and was seldom fatal."

"What an ass!" said Rulledge.

"Yes, I think he was, in this instance. But probably he had been consulted a good deal by Mrs. Ormond," said Wanhope. "The change that began to set her mind at rest about Ormond was his taking the personifications more seriously. Why, he began to ask, but always with a certain measure of joke in it, why shouldn't there be something *in* the personifications? Why shouldn't Morn and Eve come corporeally walking up their lawn, with little or no clothes on, or Despair be sitting in their woods with her hair over her face, or Famine coming gauntly up to their back door for a hand-out? Why shouldn't they any day see pop-eyed Rapture passing on the trolley, or Meditation letting the car she intended to take go by without stepping lively enough to get on board? He pretended that we could have the personifications back again, if we were not so conventional in our conceptions of them. He wanted to know what reason there was for representing Life as a very radiant and bounding party, when Life usually neither shone nor bounded; and why Death should be figured as an enemy with a dart, when it was so often the only friend a man had left, and had the habit of binding up wounds rather than inflicting them. The personifications were all right, he said, but the poets and painters did not know how they really looked. By the way," Wanhope broke off, "did you happen to see Hauptmann's 'Hannele' when it was here?"

WILLIAM DEAN HOWELLS

None of us had, and we waited rather restively for the passing of the musing fit which he fell into. After a while he resumed at a point whose relation to the matter in hand we could trace:

"It was extremely interesting for all reasons, by its absolute fearlessness and freshness in regions where there has been nothing but timid convention for a long time; but what I was thinking of was the personification of Death as it appears there. The poor little dying pauper, lying in her dream at the almshouse, sees the figure of Death. It is not the skeleton with the dart, or the phantom with the shrouded face, but a tall, beautiful young man, - as beautiful as they could get into the cast, at any rate, - clothed in simple black, and standing with his back against the mantlepiece, with his hands resting on the hilt of a long, two-handed sword. He is so quiet that you do not see him until some time after the child has seen him. When she begins to question him whether she may not somehow get to heaven without dying, he answers with a sort of sorrowful tenderness, a very sweet and noble compassion, but unsparingly as to his mission. It is a singular moment of pure poetry that makes the heart ache, but does not crush or terrify the spirit."

"And what has it got to do with Ormond?" asked Rulledge, but with less impatience than usual.

"Why, nothing, I'm afraid, that I can make out very clearly. And yet there is an obscure connection with Ormond, or his vision, if it was a vision. Mrs. Ormond could not be very definite about what he saw, perhaps because even at the last moment he was not definite himself. What she was clear about, was the fact that his mood, though it became more serious, by no means became sadder. It became a sort of solemn joy instead of the light gaiety it had begun by being. She was no sort of scientific observer, and yet the keenness of her affection made her as closely observant of Ormond as if she had been studying him psychologically. Sometimes the light in his room would wake her at night, and she would go to him, and find him lying with a book faced down on his breast, as if he had been reading, and his fingers interlaced under his head, and a kind of radiant peace in his face. The poor thing said that when she would ask him what the matter was, he would say, 'Nothing; just happiness,' and when she would ask him if he did not think he ought to do something, he would laugh, and say perhaps it would go off of itself. But it did not go off; the unnatural buoyancy continued after he became perfectly tranquil. 'I don't know,' he would say. 'I seem to have got to the end of my troubles. I haven't a care in the world, Jenny. I don't believe you could get a rise out of me if you said the nastiest thing you could think of. It sounds like nonsense, of course, but it seems to me that I have found out the reason of things, though I don't know what it is. Maybe I've only found out that there *is* a reason of things. That would be enough, wouldn't it?'"

WILLIAM DEAN HOWELLS

V.

At this point Wanhope hesitated with a kind of diffidence that was rather charming in him. "I don't see," he said, "just how I can keep the facts from this on out of the line of facts which we are not in the habit of respecting very much, or that we relegate to the company of things that are not facts at all. I suppose that in stating them I shall somehow make myself responsible for them, but that is just what I don't want to do. I don't want to do anything more than give them as they were given to me."

"You won't be able to give them half as fully," said Minver, "if Mrs. Ormond gave them to you."

"No," Wanhope said gravely, "and that's the pity of it; for they ought to be given as fully as possible."

"Go ahead," Rulledge commanded, "and do the best you can." "I'm not sure," the psychologist thoughtfully said, "that I am quite satisfied to call Ormond's experiences hallucinations. There ought to be some other word that doesn't accuse his sanity in that degree. For he apparently didn't show any other signs of an unsound mind."

"None that Mrs. Ormond would call so," Minver suggested.

"Well, in his case, I don't think she was such a bad judge,"

Wanhope returned. "She was a tolerably unbalanced person herself, but she wasn't altogether disqualified for observing him, as I've said before. They had a pretty hot summer, as the summer is apt to be in the Housatonic valley, but when it got along into September the weather was divine, and they spent nearly the whole time out of doors, driving over the hills. They got an old horse from a native, and they hunted out a rickety buggy from the carriage-house, and they went wherever the road led. They went mostly at a walk, and that suited the horse exactly, as well as Mrs. Ormond, who had no faith in Ormond's driving, and wanted to go at a pace that would give her a chance to jump out safely if anything happened. They put their hats in the front of the buggy, and went about in their bare heads. The country people got used to them, and were not scandalized by their appearance, though they were both getting a little gray, and must have looked as if they were old enough to know better.

"They were not really old, as age goes nowadays: he was not more than forty-two or -three, and she was still in the late thirties. In fact, they were

"Nel mezzo del cammin di nostra vita -

"in that hour when life, and the conceit of life, is strongest, and when it feels as if it might go on forever. Women are not very articulate about such things, and it was probably Ormond who put their feeling into words, though she recognized at once that it was her feeling, and shrank from it as if it were something wicked, that they would be punished for; so that one day, when he said suddenly, 'Jenny, I don't feel as if I could ever die,' she scolded him for it. Poor women!" said Wanhope, musingly, "they are not always cross when they scold. It is often the expression of their anxieties, their forebodings, their sex-timidities. They are always in double the danger that men are, and their nerves double that danger again. Who was that famous *salonniere* - Mme. Geoffrin, was it? - that Marmontel says always scolded her friends when they were in trouble, and came and scolded him when he was put into the Bastille? I suppose Mrs. Ormond was never so tender of Ormond as she was when she took it out of him for suggesting what she wildly felt herself, and felt she should pay for feeling."

Wanhope had the effect of appealing to Minver, but the painter would not relent. "I don't know. I've seen her - or heard her - in very devoted moments."

"At any rate," Wanhope resumed, "she says she scolded him, and it did not do the least good. She could not scold him out of that feeling, which was all mixed up in her retrospect with the sense of the weather and the season, the leaves just beginning to show the autumn, the wild asters coming to crowd the goldenrod, the crickets shrill in the grass, and the birds silent in the trees, the smell of the rowan in the meadows, and the odor of the old logs and fresh chips in the woods. She was not a woman to notice such things much, but he talked of them all and made her notice them. His nature took hold upon what we call nature, and clung fondly to the lowly and familiar aspects of it. Once she said to him, trembling for him, 'I should think you would be afraid to take such a pleasure in those things,' and when he asked her why, she couldn't or wouldn't tell him; but he understood, and he said: 'I've never realized before that I was so much a part of them. Either I am going to have them forever, or they are going to have me. We shall not part, for we are all members of the same body. If it is the body of death, we are members of that. If it is the body of life, we are members of that. Either I have never lived, or else I am never going to die.' She said: 'Of course you are never going to die; a spirit can't die.' But he told her he didn't mean that. He was just as radiantly happy when they would get home from one of their drives, and sit down to their supper, which they had country-fashion instead of dinner, and then when they would turn into their big, lamplit parlor, and sit down for a long evening with his books. Sometimes he read to her as she sewed, but he read mostly to himself, and he said he hadn't had such a bath of poetry since he was a boy. Sometimes in the splendid nights, which were so clear that you could catch the silver glint of the gossamers in the thin air, he would go out and walk up and down the long veranda. Once, when he coaxed her out with him, he took her under the arm and walked her up and down, and he said: 'Isn't it like a ship? The earth is like a ship, and we're sailing, sailing! Oh, I wonder where!' Then he stopped with a sob, and she was startled, and asked him what the matter was, but he couldn't tell her. She was more frightened than ever at what seemed a break in his happiness. She was troubled about his reading the Bible so much, especially the Old Testament; but he told her he had never known before what majestic literature it was. There were some turns or phrases in it that peculiarly took his fancy and seemed to feed it with inexhaustible suggestion. 'The Angel of the Lord' was one of these. The idea of a divine messenger, embodied and commissioned to intimate the creative will to the creature: it was sublime, it was ineffable. He wondered that men had ever come to think in any other terms of the living law that we were under, and that could much less conceivably operate like an insensate mechanism than it could reveal itself as a constant purpose. He said he believed that in every great moral crisis, in every ordeal of conscience, a man was aware of standing in the presence of something sent to try

WILLIAM DEAN HOWELLS

him and test him, and that this something was the Angel of the Lord.

"He went off that night, saying to himself, 'The Angel of the Lord, the Angel of the Lord!' and when she lay a long time awake, waiting for him to go to sleep, she heard him saying it again in his room. She thought he might be dreaming, but when she went to him, he had his lamp lighted, and was lying with that rapt smile on his face which she was so afraid of. She told him she was afraid and she wished he would not say such things; and that made him laugh, and he put his arms round her, and laughed and laughed, and said it was only a kind of swearing, and she must cheer up. He let her give him some trional to make him sleep, and then she went off to her bed again. But when they both woke late, she heard him, as he dressed, repeating fragments of verse, quoting quite without order, as the poem drifted through his memory. He told her at breakfast that it was a poem which Longfellow had written to Lowell upon the occasion of his wife's death, and he wanted to get it and read it to her. She said she did not see how he could let his mind run on such gloomy things. But he protested he was not the least gloomy, and that he supposed his recollection of the poem was a continuation of his thinking about the Angel of the Lord.

"While they were at table a tramp came up the drive under the window, and looked in at them hungrily. He was a very offensive tramp, and quite took Mrs. Ormond's appetite away: but Ormond would not send him round to the kitchen, as she wanted; he insisted upon taking him a plate and a cup of coffee out on the veranda himself. When she expostulated with him, he answered fantastically that the fellow might be an angel of the Lord, and he asked her if she remembered Parnell's poem of 'The

Hermit.' Of course she didn't, but he needn't get it, for she didn't want to hear it, and if he kept making her so nervous, she should be sick herself. He insisted upon telling her what the poem was, and how the angel in it had made himself abhorrent to the hermit by throttling the babe of the good man who had housed and fed them, and committing other atrocities, till the hermit couldn't stand it any longer, and the angel explained that he had done it all to prevent the greater harm that would have come if he had not killed and stolen in season. Ormond laughed at her disgust, and said he was curious to see what a tramp would do that was treated with real hospitality. He thought they had made a mistake in not asking this tramp in to breakfast with them; then they might have stood a chance of being murdered in their beds to save them from mischief."

WILLIAM DEAN HOWELLS

VI.

"Mrs. Ormond really lost her patience with him, and felt better than she had for a long time by scolding him in good earnest. She told him he was talking very blasphemously, and when he urged that his morality was directly in line with Parnell's, and Parnell was an archbishop, she was so vexed that she would not go to drive with him that morning, though he apologized and humbled himself in every way. He pleaded that it was such a beautiful day, it must be the last they were going to have; it was getting near the equinox, and this must be a weather-breeder. She let him go off alone, for he would not lose the drive, and she watched him out of sight from her upper window with a heavy heart. As soon as he was fairly gone, she wanted to go after him, and she was wild all the forenoon. She could not stay indoors, but kept walking up and down the piazza and looking for him, and at times she went a bit up the road he had taken, to meet him. She had got to thinking of the tramp, though the man had gone directly off down another road after he had his breakfast. At last she heard the old creaking, rattling buggy, and as soon as she saw Ormond's bare head, and knew he was all right, she ran up to her room and shut herself in. But she couldn't hold out against him when he came to her door with an armful of wild flowers that he had gathered for her, and boughs from some young maples that he had found all red in a swamp. She showed herself so interested that he asked her to come with him after their midday dinner and see them, and she said perhaps she would, if he would promise not to keep talking about the things that made her so miserable. He asked her, 'What things?' and she answered that he knew well enough, and he laughed and promised.

"She didn't believe he would keep his word, but he did at first, and he tried not to tease her in any way. He tried to please her in the whims and fancies she had about going this way or that, and when she decided not to look up his young maples with him, because the first autumn leaves made her melancholy, he submitted. He put his arm across her shoulder as they drove through the woods, and pulled her to him, and called her 'poor old thing,' and accused her of being morbid. He wanted her to tell him all there was in her mind, but she could not; she could only cry on his arm. He asked her if it was something about him that troubled her, and she could only say that she hated to see people so cheerful without reason. That made him laugh, and they were very gay after she had got her cry out; but he grew serious again. Then her temper rose, and she asked, 'Well, what is it?' and he said at first, 'Oh, nothing,' as people do when there is really something, and presently he confessed that he was thinking about what she had said of his being cheerful without reason. Then, as she said, he talked so beautifully that she had to keep her patience with him, though he was not keeping his word to her. His talk, as far as she was able to report it, didn't amount to much more than this: that in a world where death was, people never could be cheerful with reason unless death was something altogether different from what people imagined. After people came to their intellectual consciousness, death was never wholly out of it, and if they could be joyful with that black drop at the bottom of every cup, it was proof positive that death was not what it seemed. Otherwise there was no logic in the scheme of being, but it was a cruel fraud by the Creator upon the creature; a poor practical joke, with the laugh all on one side. He had got rid of his fear of it in that light, which seemed to have come to him before the fear left him, and he wanted her to see it in the same light, and if he died before her - But there she stopped him and protested that it would kill her if she did not die first, with no apparent sense, even when she told me, of her fatuity, which must have amused poor Ormond. He said what he wanted to ask was that she would believe he had not been the least afraid to die, and he wished her to remember this always, because she knew how he always used to be afraid of dying. Then he really began to talk of other things, and he led the way back to the times of their courtship and their early married days, and their first journeys together, and all their young-people friends, and the simple-hearted pleasure they used to take in society, in teas and dinners, and going to the theater. He did not like to think how that pleasure had dropped out of their life, and he did not know why they had let it, and he was going to have it again when they went to town.

"They had thought of staying a long time in the country, perhaps till after Thanksgiving, for they had become attached to their place; but now they suddenly agreed to go back to New York at once. She told me that as soon as they agreed she felt a tremendous longing to be gone that instant, as if she must go to escape from something, some calamity, and she felt, looking back, that there was a prophetic quality in her eagerness."

"Oh, she was always so," said Minver. "When a thing was to be done, she wanted it done like lightning, no matter what the thing was."

"Well, very likely," Wanhope consented. "I never make

much account of those retroactive forebodings. At any rate, she says she wanted him to turn about and drive home so that they could begin packing, and when he demurred, and began to tease, as she called it, she felt as if she should scream, till he turned the old horse and took the back track. She was *wild* to get home, and kept hurrying him, and wanting him to whip the horse; but the old horse merely wagged his tail, and declined to go faster than a walk, and this was the only thing that enabled her to forgive herself afterward."

"Why, what had she done?" Rulledge asked. "She would have been responsible for what happened, according to her notion, if she had had her way with the horse; she would have felt that she had driven Ormond to his doom."

"Of course!" said Minver. "She always found a hole to creep out of. Why couldn't she go back a little further, and hold herself responsible through having made him turn round?"

"Poor woman!" said Rulledge, with a tenderness that made Minver smile. "What was it that did happen?"

Wanhope examined his cup for some dregs of coffee, and then put it down with an air of resignation. I offered to touch the bell, but, "No, don't," he said. "I'm better without it." And he went on: "There was a lonely piece of woods that they had to drive through before they struck the avenue leading to their house, which was on a cheerful upland overlooking the river, and when they had got about half-way through this woods, the tramp whom Ormond had fed in the morning, slipped out of a thicket on the hillside above them, and crossed the road in front of them, and slipped out of sight among the trees on the slope below. Ormond stopped the horse, and turned to his wife with a strange kind of whisper. 'Did you see it?' he asked, and she answered yes, and bade him drive on. He did so, slowly looking back round the side of the buggy till a turn of the road hid the place where the tramp had crossed their track. She could not speak, she says, till they came in sight of their house. Then her heart gave a great bound, and she broke out on him, blaming him for having encouraged the tramp to lurk about, as he must have done, all day, by his foolish sentimentality in taking his breakfast out to him. 'He saw that you were a delicate person, and now to-night he will be coming round, and - ' She says Ormond kept looking at her, while she talked, as if he did not know what she was saying, and all at once she glanced down at their feet, and discovered that her hat was gone.

"That, she owned, made her frantic, and she blazed out at him again, and accused him of having lost her hat by stopping to look at that worthless fellow, and then starting up the horse so suddenly that it had rolled out. He usually gave her as good as she sent when she let herself go in that way, and she told me she would have been glad if he had done it now, but he only looked at her in a kind of daze, and when he understood, at last, he bade her get out and go into the house - they were almost at the door, - and he would go back and find her hat himself. 'Indeed, you'll do nothing of the kind,' she said she told him. 'I shall go back with you, or you'll be hunting up that precious vagabond and bringing him home to supper.' Ormond said, 'All right,' with a kind of dreamy passivity, and he turned the old horse again, and they drove slowly back, looking for the hat in the road, right and left. She had not noticed before that it was getting late, and perhaps it was not so late as it seemed when they got into that lonely piece of woods again, and the veils of shadow began to drop round them, as if they were something falling from the trees, she said. They found the hat easily enough at the point where it must have rolled out of the buggy, and he got down and picked it up. She kept scolding him, but he did not seem to hear her. He stood dangling the hat by its ribbons from his right hand, while he rested his left on the dashboard, and looking - looking down into the wooded slope where the tramp had disappeared. A cold chill went over her, and she stopped her scolding. 'Oh, Jim,' she said, 'do you see something? What do you see?' He flung the hat from him, and ran plunging down the hillside - she covered up her face when she told me, and said she should always see him running - till the dusk among the trees hid him. She ran after him, and she heard him calling, calling joyfully, 'Yes, I'm coming!' and she thought he was calling back to her, but the rush of his feet kept getting farther, and then he seemed to stop with a sound like falling. He couldn't have been much ahead of her, for it was only a moment till she stood on the edge of a boulder in the woods, looking over, and there at the bottom Ormond was lying with his face turned under him, as she expressed it; and the tramp, with a heavy stick in his hand, was standing by him, stooping over him, and staring at him. She began to scream, and it seemed to her that she flew down from the brink of the rock, and caught the tramp and clung to him, while she kept screaming 'Murder!' The man didn't try to get away; he only said, over and over, 'I didn't touch him, lady; I didn't touch him.' It all happened simultaneously, like events in a dream, and while there was nobody there but herself and the tramp, and Ormond lying between them, there were some people that must have heard her from the road and come down to her. They were neighbor-folk that knew her and Ormond, and they naturally laid hold of the tramp; but he didn't try to escape. He helped them gather poor Ormond up, and he went back to the house with them, and staid while one of them ran for the doctor. The doctor

WILLIAM DEAN HOWELLS

could only tell them that Ormond was dead, and that his neck must have been broken by his fall over the rock. One of the neighbors went to look at the place the next morning, and found one of the roots of a young tree growing on the rock, torn out, as if Ormond had caught his foot in it; and that had probably made his fall a headlong dive. The tramp knew nothing but that he heard shouting and running, and got up from the foot of the rock, where he was going to pass the night, when something came flying through the air, and struck at his feet. Then it scarcely stirred, and the next thing, he said, the lady was *onto* him, screeching and tearing. He piteously protested his innocence, which was apparent enough, at the inquest, and before, for that matter. He said Ormond was about the only man that ever treated him white, and Mrs. Ormond was remorseful for having let him get away before she could tell him that she didn't blame him, and ask him to forgive her."

VII.

Wanhope desisted with a provisional air, and Rulledge went and got Himself a sandwich from the lunch-table.

"Well, upon my word!" said Minver. "I thought you had dined, Rulledge."

Rulledge came back munching, and said to Wanhope, as he settled himself in his chair again: "Well, go on."

"Why, that's all."

The psychologist was silent, with Rulledge staring indignantly at him.

"I suppose Mrs. Ormond had her theory?" I ventured.

"Oh, yes - such as it was," said Wanhope. "It was her belief - her religion - that Ormond had seen Death, in person or personified, or the angel of it; and that the sight was something beautiful, and not terrible. She thought that she should see Death, too in the same way, as a messenger. I don't know that it was such a bad theory," he added impartially.

"Not," said Minver, "if you suppose that Ormond was off his nut. But, in regard to the whole matter, there is always a question of how much truth there was in what she said about it."

"Of course," the psychologist admitted, "that is a question which must be considered. The question of testimony in such matters is the difficult thing. You might often believe in supernatural occurrences if it were not for the witnesses. It is very interesting," he pursued, with his scientific smile, "to note how corrupting anything supernatural or mystical is. Such things seem mostly to happen either in the privity of people who are born liars, or else they deprave the spectator so, through his spiritual vanity or his love of the marvelous, that you can't believe a word he says.

"They are as bad as horses on human morals," said Minver. "Not that I think it ever needed the coming of a ghost to invalidate any statement of Mrs. Ormond's." Rulledge rose and went away growling something, partially audible, to the disadvantage of Minver's wit, and the painter laughed after him: "He really believes it."

Wanhope's mind seemed to be shifted from Mrs. Ormond to her convert, whom he followed with his tolerant eyes. "Nothing in all this sort of inquiry is so impossible to predicate as the effect of any given instance upon a given mind. It would be very interesting - "

"Excuse me!" said Minver. "There's Whitley. I must speak to him."

He went away, leaving me alone with the psychologist.

"And what is your own conclusion in this instance?" I asked.

"Why, I haven't formulated it yet."

THOUGH ONE ROSE FROM THE DEAD.

I.

You are very welcome to the Alderling incident, my dear
Acton, if you think you can do anything with it, and I will
give it as circumstantially as possible. The thing has its
limitations, I should think, for the fictionist, chiefly in a
sort of roundedness which leaves little play to the
imagination. It seems to me that it would be more to your
purpose if it were less *pat*, in its catastrophe, but you are a
better judge of all that than I am, and I will put the facts in
your hands, and keep my own hands off, so far as any
plastic use of the material is concerned.

The first I knew of the peculiar Alderling situation was
shortly after William James's "Will to Believe" came out.
I had been telling the Alderlings about it, for they had not
seen it, and I noticed that from time to time they looked
significantly at each other. When I had got through he
gave a little laugh, and she said, "Oh, you may laugh!"
and then I made bold to ask, "What is it?"

"Marion can tell you," he said. He motioned towards the
coffee-pot and asked, "More?" I shook my head, and he
said, "Come out and let us see what the maritime interests
have been doing for us. Pipe or cigar?" I chose cigarettes,

WILLIAM DEAN HOWELLS

and he brought the box off the table, stopping on his way to the veranda, and taking his pipe and tobacco-pouch from the hall mantel.

Mrs. Alderling had got to the veranda before us, and done things to the chairs and cushions, and was leaning against one of the slender fluted pine columns like some rich, blond caryatid just off duty, with the blue of her dress and the red of her hair showing deliciously against the background of white house-wall. He and she were an astonishing and satisfying contrast; in the midst of your amazement you felt the divine propriety of a woman like her wanting just such a wiry, smoky-complexioned, black-browed, black-bearded, bald-headed little man as he was. Before he sat down where she was going to put him, he stood stoopingly, and frowned at the waters of the cove lifting from the foot of the lawn that sloped to it before the house. "Three lumbermen, two goodish-sized yachts, a dozen sloop-rigged boats: not so bad. About the usual number that come loafing in to spend the night. You ought to see them when it threatens to breeze up. Then they're here in flocks. Go on, Marion."

He gave a soft groan of comfort as he settled in his chair and began pulling at his short black pipe, and she let her eyes dwell on him in a rapture that curiously interested me. People in love are rarely interesting - that is, flesh-and-blood people. Of course I know that lovers are the life of fiction, and that a story of any kind can scarcely hold the reader without them. The love-interest, as they call it, is also supposed to be essential to the drama, and friends of mine who have tried to foist their plays upon managers have been overthrown by the objection that the love-interest is not strong enough in what they have done. Yet lovers in real life are, so far as I have observed them, bores. They are confessed to be disgusting before or after marriage when they let their fondness appear, but even when they try to hide it, they are tiresome. Character goes down before passion in them; nature is reduced to propensity. Then, how is it that the novelist manages to keep these, and to give us nature and character while seeming to offer nothing but propensity and passion? Perhaps he does not give them. Perhaps what he does is to hypnotize us so that we each of us identify ourselves with the lovers, and add our own natures and characters to the single principle that animates them. The reason we like, that we endure, to read about them, may be that they are ourselves rendered objective in an instant of intense vitality, without the least trouble or risk to us. But if we have them there before us in the tiresome reality, they exclude us from their pleasure in each other and stop up the perspective of our happiness with their hulking personalities, bare of all the iridescence of potentiality, which we could have cast about them. Something of this iridescence may cling to unmarried lovers, in spite of themselves, but wedded bliss is a sheer offence.

I do not know why it was not an offence in the case of the Alderlings, unless it was because they both, in their different ways, saw the joke of the thing. At any rate, I found that in their charm for each other they had somehow not ceased to be amusing for me, and I waited confidently for the answer she would make to his whimsically abrupt bidding. But she did not answer very promptly, even when he had added, "Wanhope, here, is scenting something psychological in the reason of my laughing at you, instead of accepting the plain inference in the case."

"What is the plain inference?" I asked, partly to fill up Mrs. Alderling's continued silence.

"When a man laughs at a woman for no apparent reason it is because he is amused at her being afraid of him when he is so much more afraid of her, or puzzled by him when she is such an incomparable riddle herself, or caring for him when he knows he is not worth his salt."

"You don't expect to put me off with that sort of thing," I said.

"Well, then, go on Marion," Alderling repeated.

II.

Mrs. Alderling stood looking at him, not me, with a smile hovering about the corners of her mouth, which, when it decided not to alight anywhere, scarcely left her aspect graver for its flitting. She said at last, in her slow, deep-throated voice, "I guess I will let you tell him."

"Oh, I'll tell him fast enough," said Alderling, nursing his knee, and bringing it well up toward his chin, between his clasped hands. "Marion has always had the notion that I should live again if I believed I should, and that as I don't believe I shall, I am not going to. The joke of it is," and he began to splutter laughter round the stem of his pipe, "she's as much of an agnostic as I am. She doesn't believe she is going to live again, either."

Mrs. Alderling said, "I don't care for it in my case." That struck me as rather touching, but I had no right to enter uninvited into the intimacy of her meaning, and I said, looking as little at her as I need, "Aren't you both rather belated?"

"You mean that protoplasm has gone out?" he chuckled.

"Not exactly," I answered. "But you know that a great many things are allowed now that were once forbidden to the True Disbeliever."

"You mean that we may trust in the promises, as they used to be called, and still keep the Unfaith?"

"Something like that."

Alderling took his pipe out, apparently to give his whole face to the pleasure of teasing his wife.

"That'll be a great comfort to Marion," he said, and he threw back his head and laughed.

She smiled faintly, vaguely, tolerantly, as if she enjoyed his pleasure in teasing her.

"Where have you been," I asked, "that you don't know the changed attitude in these matters?"

"Well, here for the last three years. We tried it the first winter after we came, and found it was not so bad, and we simply stayed on. But I haven't really looked into the question since I gave the conundrum up twenty years ago, on what was then the best authority. Marion doesn't complain. She knew what I was when she married me. She was another. We were neither of us very bigoted disbelievers. We should not have burned anybody at the stake for saying that we had souls."

Alderling put back his pipe and cackled round it, taking his knee between his hands again.

"You know," she explained, more in my direction than to me, "that I had none to begin with. But Alderling had. His people believed in the future life."

"That's what they said," Alderling crowed. "And Marion has always thought that if she had believed that way, she could have kept me up to it; and so when I died I should have lived again. It is perfectly logical, though it isn't capable of a practical demonstration. If Marion had come of a believing family, she could have brought me back into the fold. Her great mistake was in being brought up by an uncle who denied that he was living here, even. The poor girl could not do a thing when it came to the life hereafter."

The smile now came hovering back, and alighted at a corner of Mrs. Alderling's mouth, making it look, oddly enough, rather rueful. "It didn't matter about me. I thought it a pity that Alderling's talent should stop here."

"Did you ever know anything like that?" he cried. "Perfectly willing to thrust me out into a cold other-world, and leave me to struggle on without her, when I had got used to her looking after me. Now I'm not so selfish as that. I shouldn't want to have Marion living on through all eternity if I wasn't with her. It would be too lonely for her."

He looked up at her, with his dancing eyes, and she put her hand down over his shoulder into the hand that he lifted to meet it, in a way that would have made me sick in some people. But in her the action was so casual, so absent, that it did not affect me disagreeably.

"Do you mean that you haven't been away since you came here three years ago?" I asked.

"We ran up to the theatre once in Boston last winter, but it bored us to the limit." Alderling poked his knife-blade into the bowl of his pipe as he spoke, having freed his hand for the purpose, while Mrs. Alderling leaned back against the slim column again. He said gravely: "It was a great thing for Marion, though. In view of the railroad accident that didn't happen, she convinced herself that her sole ambition was that we should die together. Then, whether we found ourselves alive or not, we should be company for each other. She's got it arranged with the thunderstorms, so that one bolt will do for us both, and she never lets me go out on the water alone, for fear I shall watch my chance, and get drowned without her."

I did not trouble myself to make out how much of this was mocking, and as there was no active participation in the joke expected of me, I kept on the safe side of laughing. "No wonder you've been able to do such a lot of pictures," I said. "But I should have thought you might have found it dull - I mean dull together - at odd times."

"Dull?" he shouted. "It's stupendously dull! Especially when our country neighbors come in to "liven us up.' We've got neighbors here that can stay longer in half an hour than most people can in a week. We get tired of each other at times, but after a call from the people in the next house, we return with rapture to our delusion that we are interesting."

"And you never," I ventured, making my jocosity as ironical as possible, "wear upon each other?"

"Horribly!" said Alderling, and his wife smiled contentedly, behind him. "We haven't a whole set of china in the house, from exchanging it across the table, and I haven't made a study of Marion - you must have noticed how many Marions there were that she hasn't thrown at my head. Especially the Madonnas. She likes to throw the Madonnas at me."

I ventured still farther, addressing myself to Mrs.

Alderling. "Does he keep it up all the time - this blague?"

"Pretty much," she answered passively, with entire acquiescence in the fact if it were the fact, or the joke if it were the joke.

"But I didn't see anything of yours, Mrs. Alderling," I said. She had had her talent, as a girl, and some people preferred it to her husband's, - but there was no effect of it anywhere in the house.

"The housekeeping is enough," she answered, with her tranquil smile.

There was nothing in her smile that was leading, and I did not push my inquiry, especially as Alderling did not seem disposed to assist. "Well," I said, "I suppose you will forgive to science my feeling that your situation is most suggestive."

"Oh, don't mind *us!*" said Alderling.

"I won't, thank you," I answered. "Why, it's equal to being cast away together on an uninhabited island."

"Quite," he assented.

"There can't," I went on, "be a corner of your minds that you haven't mutually explored. You must know each other," I cast about for the word, and added abruptly, "by heart."

"I don't suppose he meant anything pretty?" said Alderling, with a look up over his shoulder at his wife; and then he said to me, "We do; and there are some very curious things I could tell you, if Marion would ever let me get in a word."

"Do let him, Mrs. Alderling," I entreated, humoring his joke at her silence.

She smiled, and softly shrugged, and then sighed.

"I could make your flesh creep," he went on, "or I could if you were not a psychologist. I assure you that we are quite weird at times."

"As how?"

"Oh, just knowing what the other is thinking, at a given moment, and saying it. There are times when Marion's thinking is such a nuisance to me, that I have to yell down to her from my loft to stop it. The racket it makes breaks me all up. It's a relief to have her talk, and I try to make her, when she's posing, just to escape the din of her thinking. Then the willing! We experimented with it, after we had first noticed it, but we don't any more. It's too dead easy."

"What do you mean by the willing?" I asked.

"Oh, just wishing one that the other was there, and there he or she is."

"Is he trying to work me, Mrs. Alderling?" I appealed to her, and she answered from her calm:

"It is very unaccountable."

"Then you really mean it! Why can't you give me an illustration?"

"Why, you know," said Alderling more seriously than he had yet spoken, "I don't believe those things, if they are real, can ever be got to show off. That's the reason why your 'Quests in the Occult' are mainly such rubbish, as far as the evidences are concerned. If Marion and I tried to give you an illustration, as you call it, the occult would snub us. But, is there anything so very strange about it? The wonder *is* that a man and wife ever fail of knowing each what the other is thinking. They pervade each other's minds, if they are really married, and they are so present with each other that the tacit wish should be the same as a call. Marion and I are only an intensified instance of what may be done by living together. There is something, though, that is rather queer, but it belongs to psycho-mancy rather than psychology, as I understand it."

"Ah!" I said. "What is that queer something?"

"Being visibly present when absent. It has not happened often, but it has happened that I have seen Marion in my loft when she was really somewhere else and not when I had willed her or wished her to be there."

"Now, really," I said, "I must ask you for an instance."

"You want to heap up facts, Lombroso fashion? Well, this is as good as most of Lombroso's facts, or better. I went up one morning, last winter, to work at a study of a Madonna from Marion, directly after breakfast, and left her below in the dining-room, putting away the breakfast things. She has to do that occasionally, between the local helps, who are all we can get in the winter. She professes to like it, but you never can tell, from what a woman says; she has to do it, anyway." It is hard to convey a notion of the serene, impersonal acquiescence of Mrs. Alderling in taking this talk of her. "I was banging away at it when I knew she was behind me looking over my shoulder rather more stormily than she usually does; usually, she is a dead calm. I glanced up, and saw the calm succeed the storm. I kept on, and after awhile I was aware of hearing her step on the stairs."

Alderling stopped, and smoked definitively, as if that were the end.

"Well," I said, after waiting a while, "I don't exactly get the unique value of the incident."

"Oh," he said, as if he had accidentally forgotten the detail, "the steps were coming up?"

"Yes?"

"She opened the door, which she had omitted to do before, and when she came in she denied having been there already. She owned that she had been hurrying through her work, and thinking of mine, so as to make me do something, or undo something, to it; and then all at once she lost her impatience, and came up at her leisure. I don't exactly like to tell what she wanted."

He began to laugh provokingly, and she said, tranquilly, "I don't mind your telling Mr. Wanhope."

"Well, then, strictly in the interest of psychomancy, I will confide that she had found some traces of a model that I used to paint my Madonnas from, before we were married, in that picture. She had slept on her suspicion, and then when she could not stand it any longer, she had come up in the spirit to say that she was not going to be mixed up in a Madonna with any such minx. The words are mine, but the meaning was Marion's. When she found me taking the minx out, she went quietly back to washing her dishes, and then returned in the body to give me a sitting."

WILLIAM DEAN HOWELLS

III.

We were silent a moment, till I asked, "Is this true, Mrs. Alderling?"

"About," she said. "I don't remember the storm, exactly."

"Well, I don't see why you bother to remain in the body at all," I remarked.

"We haven't arranged just how to leave it together," said Alderling. "Marion, here, if I managed to get off first, would have no means of knowing whether her theory of the effect of my unbelief on my future was right or not; and if *she* gave *me* the slip, she would always be sorry that she had not stayed here to convert me."

"Why don't you agree that if either of you lives again, he or she shall make some sign to let the other know?" I suggested. "Well, that has been tried so often, and has it ever worked? It's open to the question whether the dead do not fail to show up because they are forbidden to communicate with the living; and you are just where you were, as to the main point. No, I don't see any way out of it."

Mrs. Alderling went into the house and came out with a book in her hand, and her fingers in it at two places. It was that impressive collection of Christ's words from the

New Testament called "The Great Discourse." She put the book before me, first at one place and then at another, and I read, "Whosoever liveth and believeth in me shall never die," and then, "Nay, but except ye repent, ye shall all likewise perish." She did not say anything in showing me these passages, and I found something in her action touchingly childlike and elemental, as well as curiously heathenish. It was as if some poor pagan had brought me his fetish to test its effect upon me. "Yes," I said, "those are things that we hardly know what to do with in our philosophy. They seem to be said as with authority, and yet, somehow, we cannot admit their validity in a philosophical inquiry as to a future life. Aren't they generally taken to mean that we shall be unhappy or happy hereafter, rather than that we shall be or not be at all? And what is believing? Is it the mere act of acknowledgement, or is it something more vital, which expresses itself in conduct?"

She did not try to say. In fact she did not answer at all. Whatever point was in her mind she did not, or could not, debate it. I perceived, in a manner, that her life was so largely subliminal that if she had tried she could not have met my question any more than if she had not had the gift of speech at all. But, in her inarticulate fashion, she had exposed to me a state of mind which I was hardly withheld by the decencies from exploring. "You know," I said, "that psychology almost begins by rejecting the authority of these sayings, and that while we no longer deny anything, we cannot allow anything merely because it has been strongly affirmed. Supposing that there is a life after this, how can it be denied to one and bestowed upon another because one has assented to a certain supernatural claim and another has refused to do so? That does not seem reasonable, it does not seem right. Why should you base your conclusion as to that life upon a promise and a menace which may not really refer to it in the sense which they seem to have?"

"Isn't it all there is?" she asked, and Alderling burst into his laugh.

"I'm afraid she's got you there, Wanhope. When it comes to polemics there's nothing like the passive obstruction of Mrs. Alderling. Marion might never have been an early Christian herself - I think she's an inexpugnable pagan - but she would have gone round making it awfully uncomfortable for the other unbelievers."

"You know," she said to him, and I never could decide how much she was in earnest, "that I can't believe till you do. I couldn't take the risk of keeping on without you."

Alderling followed her in-doors, where she now went to put the book away, with the mock addressed to me, "Did you ever know such a stubborn woman?"

IV.

One conclusion from my observation of the Alderlings during the week I spent with them was that it is bad for a husband and wife to be constantly and unreservedly together, not because they grow tired of each other, but because they grow more intensely interested in each other. Children, when they come, serve the purpose of separating the parents; they seem to unite them in one care, but they divide them in their employments, at least in the normally constituted family. If they are rich, and can throw the care of the children upon servants, then they cannot enjoy the relief from each other that children bring to the mother who nurtures and teaches them, and to the father who must work for them harder than before. The Alderlings were not rich enough to have been freed from the wholesome responsibilities of parentage, but they were childless, and so they were not detached from the perpetual thought of each other. If they had only had different tastes, it might have been better, but they were both artists, she not less than he, though she no longer painted. When their common thoughts were not centred upon each other's being, they were centred on his work, which, viciously enough, was the constant reproduction of her visible personality. I could always see them studying each other, he with an eye to her beauty, she with an eye to his power.

He was every now and then saying to her, "Hold on,

Marion," and staying her in some pose or movement, while he made mental note of it, and I was conscious of her preying upon his inmost thoughts and following him into the recesses of his reveries, where it is best for a man to be alone, even if he is sometimes a beast there. She was not like those wives who ask their husbands, when they do not happen to be talking, "What are you thinking about?" and I put this to her credit, till I realized that she had no need to ask, for she knew already. Now and then I saw him get up and shake himself restively, but I am bound to say in her behalf, that her pursuit of him seemed quite involuntary, and that she enjoyed it no more than he did. Twenty times I was on the point of asking, "Why don't you people go in for a good long separation? Is there nothing to call you to Europe, Alderling? Haven't you got a mother, or sister, or some one that you could visit, Mrs. Alderling? It would do you both a world of good."

But it happened, oddly enough, that the Alderlings were as kinless as they were childless, and if he had gone to Europe he would have taken her with him, and prolonged their seclusion by the isolation in which people necessarily live in a foreign country. I found I was the only acquaintance who had visited them during the years of their retirement on the coast, where they had stayed, partly through his inertia, and partly from his superstition that he could paint better away from the ordinary associations and incentives; and they ceased, before I left, to get the good they might of my visit because they made me a part of their intimacy, instead of making themselves part of my strangeness.

After a day or two, their queer experiences began to resume themselves, unabashed by my presence. These were mostly such as they had already more than hinted to me: the thought-transferences, and the unconscious hypnotic suggestions which they made to each other. There was more novelty in the last than the first. If I could trust them, and they did not seem to wish to exploit their mysteries for the effect on me, they were with each other because one or the other had willed it. She would say, if we were sitting together without him, "I think Rupert wants me; I'll be back in a moment," and he, if she were not by, for some time, would get up with, "Excuse me, I must go to Marion; she's calling me."

I had to take a great deal of this on faith; in fact, none of it was susceptible of proof; but I have not been able since to experience all the skepticism which usually replaces the impression left by sympathy with such supposed occurrences. The thing was not quite what we call uncanny; the people were so honest, both of them, that the morbid character of like situations was wanting. The events, if they could be called so, were not invited, I was quite sure, and they were varied by such diversions as we had in reach. I went blueberrying with Mrs. Alderling in the morning after she had got her breakfast dishes put away, in order that we might have something for dessert at our midday dinner; and I went fishing off the old stone crib with Alderling in the afternoon, so that we might have cunners for supper. The farmerfolks and fisherfolks seemed to know them and to be on tolerant terms with them, though it was plain that they still considered them probational in their fellow-citizenship. I do not think they were liked the less because they did not assume to be of the local sort, but let their difference stand, if it would. There was nothing countrified in her dress, which was frankly conventional; the short walking-skirt had as sharp a slant in front as her dinner-gown would have had, and he wore his knickerbockers - it was then the now-faded hour of knickerbockers - with an air of going out golfing in the suburbs. They stood on ceremony in addressing the natives, who might have been Jim or Liza to each other, but were always Mr. Donald or Mrs. Moody, with the Alderlings. They said they would not like being called by their first names themselves, and they did not see why they should take that freedom with others. Neither by nature nor by nurture were they out of the ordinary in their ideals, and it was by a sort of accident that they were so different in their realities. She had stayed on with him through the first winter in the place they had taken for the summer, because she wished to be with him, rather than because she wished to be there, and he had stayed because he had not just found the moment to break away, though afterwards he pretended a reason for staying. They had no more voluntarily cultivated the natural than the super-natural; he kindled the fire for her, and she made the coffee for him, not because they preferred, but because they must; and they had arrived at their common ground in the occult by virtue of being alone together, and not by seeking the solitude for the experiment which the solitude promoted. Mrs. Alderling did not talk less, nor he more, when either was alone with me, than when we were all together; perhaps he was more silent, and she not quite so much; she was making up for him in his absence as he was for her in her presence. But they were always hospitable and attentive hosts, and though under the peculiar circumstances of Mrs. Alderling's having to do the house-work I necessarily had to do a good many things for myself, there were certain little graces which were never wanting, from her hands: my curtains were always carefully drawn, and my coverlet triangularly opened, so that I did not have to pull it down myself. There was a freshly trimmed lamp on the stand at my bed-head, and a book and paper-cutter put there, with a decanter of whiskey and a glass of water. I note these things to you, because they are touches which help remove the sense of anything intentional in the occultism of the Alderlings.

I do not know whether I shall be able to impart the feeling of an obscure pathos in the case of Mrs. Alderling, which I certainly did not experience in Alderling's. Temperamentally he was less fitted to undergo the rigors of their seclusion than she was; in his liking to talk, he needed an audience and a variety of listening, and she, in her somewhat feline calm, could not have been troubled by any such need. You can be silent to yourself, but you cannot very well be loquacious, without danger of having the devil for a listener, if the old saying is true. Yet still, I felt a keener poignancy in her sequestration. Her beauty had even greater claim to regard than his eloquence. She was a woman who could have commanded a whole roomful with it, and no one would have wanted a word from her. She could only have been entirely herself in society, where, and in spite of everything that can be said against it, we can each, if we will, be more natural than out of it. The reason that most of us are not natural in it is that we want to play parts for which we are more or less unfit, and Marion Alderling never wished to play a part, I was sure. It would have sufficed her to be herself wherever she was, and the more people there were by, the more easily she could have been herself.

I am not able to say now how much of all this is observation of previous facts, and how much speculation based upon subsequent occurrences. At the best I can only let it stand for characterization. In the same interest I will add a fact in relation to Mrs. Alderling which ought to have its weight against any undue appeal I have been making in her behalf. Without in the least blaming her, I will say that I think that Mrs. Alderling ate too much. She must have had naturally a strong appetite, which her active life sharpened, and its indulgence formed a sort of refuge from the pressure of the intense solitude in which she lived, and which was all the more a solitude because it was *solitude a deux*. I noticed that beyond the habit of cooks she partook of the dishes she had prepared, and that after Alderling and I had finished dinner, and he was impatient to get at his pipe, she remained prolonging her dessert. One night, when he and I came in from the veranda, she was standing at the sideboard, bent over a saucer of something, and she made me think of a large tortoise-shell cat which has got at the cream. I expected in my nerves to hear her lap, and my expectation was heightened by the soft, purring laugh with which she owned that she was hungry, and those berries were so nice.

At the risk of giving the effect of something sensuous, even sensual, in her, I find myself insisting upon this detail, which did not lessen her peculiar charm. As far as the mystical quality of the situation was concerned, I fancy your finding that rather heightened by her innocent *gourmandise*. You must have noticed how inextricably, for this life at least, the spiritual is trammeled in the material, how personal character and ancestral propensity seem to flow side by side in the same individual without necessarily affecting each other. On the moral side Mrs. Alderling was no more to be censured for the refuge which her nerves sought from the situation in over-eating than Alderling for the smoking in which he escaped from the pressure they both felt from one another; and she was not less fitted than he for their joint experience.

V.

I do not suppose it was with the notion of keeping her
weight down that Mrs. Alderling rowed a good deal on
the cove before the cottage; but she had a boat, which she
managed very well, and which she was out in, pretty
much the whole time when she was not cooking, or eating
or sleeping, or roaming the berry-pastures with me, or
sitting to Alderling for his Madonnas. He did not care for
the water himself; he said he knew every inch of that
cove, and was tired of it; but he rather liked his wife's
going, and they may both have had an unconscious relief
from each other in the absences which her excursions
promoted. She swam as well as she rowed, and often we
saw her going down water-proofed to the shore, where we
presently perceived her pulling off in her bathing-dress.
Well out in the cove she had the habit of plunging
overboard, and after a good swim, she rowed back, and
then, discreetly water-proofed again, she climbed the
lawn back to the house. Now and then she took me out in
her boat, but so far as I remember, Alderling never went
with her. Once I ventured to ask him if he never felt
anxious about her. He said no, he should not have been
afraid to go with her, and she could take better care of
herself than he could. Besides, by means of their telepathy
they were in constant communion, and he could make her
feel at any sort of chance, that he did not wish her to take
it, and she would not. This was the only occasion when he
treated their peculiar psychomancy boastfully, and the

only occasion when I felt a distinct misgiving of his sincerity.

The day before I left, Mrs. Alderling went down about eleven in the morning to her boat, and rowed out into the cove. She rowed far toward the other shore, whither, following her with my eyes from Alderling's window, I saw its ridge blotted out by a long low cloud. It was straight and level as a wall, and looked almost as dense, and I called Alderling.

"Oh, that fog won't come in before afternoon," he said. "We usually get it about four o'clock. But even if it does," he added dreamily, "Marion can manage. I'd trust her anywhere in this cove in any kind of weather."

He went back to his work, and painted away for five or six minutes. Then he asked me, still at the window, "What's that fog doing now?"

"Well, I don't know," I answered. "I should say it was making in."

"Do you see Marion?"

"Yes, she seems to be taking her bath."

Again he painted a while before he asked, "Has she had her dip?"

"She's getting back into her boat."

"All right," said Alderling, in a tone of relief. "She's good to beat any fog in these parts ashore. I wish you would come and look at this a minute."

I went, and we lost ourselves for a time in our criticism of the picture. He was harder on it than I was. He allowed, *"C'est un bon portrait,* as the French used to say of a faithful landscape, though I believe now the portrait can't be too good for them. I can't say about landscape. But in a Madonna I feel that there can be too much Marion, not for me, of course, but for the ideal, which I suppose we are bound to respect. Marion is not spiritual, but I would not have her less of the earth earthy, for all the angels that ever spread themselves 'in strong level flight.'"

I recognized the words from "The Blessed Damozel," and I made bold to be so personal as to say, "If her hair were a little redder than 'the color of ripe corn' one might almost feel that the Blessed Damozel had been painted from Mrs. Alderling. It's the lingering earthiness in her that makes the Damozel so divine."

"Yes, that was a great conception. I wonder none of the fellows do that kind of thing now."

I laughed and said, "Well, so few of them have had the advantage of seeing Mrs. Alderling. And besides, Rosettis don't happen every day."

"It was the period, too. I always tell her that she belongs among the later eighteen sixties. But she insists that she wasn't even born then. Marion is tremendously single-minded."

"She has her mind all on you."

He looked askance at me. "You've noticed - "

"I've noticed that your mind is all on her."

"Not half as much!" he protested, fervidly. "I don't think it's good for her, though of course I like it. That is, in a way. Sometimes it's rather too - " He suddenly flung his brush from him, and started up, with a loudly shouted, "Yes, yes! I'm coming," and hurled himself out of the garret which he used for his studio, and cleared the stairs with two bounds.

By the time I reached the outer door of the cottage, he was a dark blur in the white blur of the fog which had swallowed up the cove, and was rising round the house-walls from the grass. I heard him shouting, "Marion!" and a faint mellow answer, far out in the cove, "Hello!" and then -

"Where are you?" and her answer "Here!" I heard him jump into a boat, and the thump of the oars in the row-locks, and then the rapid beat of the oars while he shouted, "Keep calling!" and she answered, -

"I will!" and called "Hello! Hello! Hello!"

I made my mental comment that this time their mystical means of communication was somehow not working. But after her last hello, no sound broke the white silence of the fog except the throb of Alderling's oars. She was evidently resting on hers, lest she should baffle his attempts to find her by trying to find him.

I suppose ten minutes or so had passed, when the dense air brought me the sound of low laughing that was also like the sound of low sobbing, and then I knew that they had met somewhere in the blind space. I began to hear rowing again, but only as of one boat, and suddenly out of the mist, almost at my feet, Alderling's boat shot up on the shelving beach, and his wife leaped ashore from it, and ran past me up the lawn, while he pulled her boat out on the gravel. She must have been trailing it from the stern of his.

VI.

I was abroad when Mrs. Alderling died, but I heard that it was from a typhoid fever which she had contracted from the water in their well, as was supposed. The water-supply all along that coast is scanty, and that summer most of the wells were dry, and quite a plague of typhoid raged among the people from drinking the dregs. The fever might have gone the worse with her because of her over-fed robustness; at any rate it went badly enough.

I first heard of her death from Minver at the club, and I heard with still greater astonishment that Alderling was down there alone where she had died. Minver said that somebody ought to go down and look after the poor old fellow, but nobody seemed to feel it exactly his office. Certainly I did not feel it mine, and I thought it rather a hardship when a few days after I found a letter from Alderling at the club quite piteously beseeching me to come to him. He had read of my arrival home, in a stray New York paper, and he was firing his letter, he said, at the club, with one chance in a thousand of hitting me with it. Rulledge was by when I read it, and he decided, with that unsparing activity of his, where other people are concerned, that I must go; I certainly could not resist such an appeal as that. He had a vague impression, he said, of something weird in the situation down there, and I ought to go and pull Alderling out of it; besides, I might find my account in it as a psychologist. I hesitated a day, out of self-respect, or self-assertion, and then, the weather coming on suddenly hot, in the beginning of September, I went.

Of course I had meant to go, all along, but I was not so glad when I arrived, as I might have been if Alderling had given me a little warmer welcome. His mood had changed since writing to me, and the strongest feeling he showed at seeing me was what affected me very like a cold surprise.

If I had broken in on a solitude in that place before, I was now the intruder upon a desolation. Alderling was living absolutely alone, except for the occasional presence of a neighboring widow - all the middle-aged women there are widows, with dim or dimmer memories of husbands lost off the Banks, or elsewhere at sea - who came in to get his meals and make his bed, and then had instructions to leave. It was in one of her prevailing absences that I arrived with my bag, and I had to hammer a long time with the knocker on the open door before Alderling came clacking down the stairs in his slippers from the top of the house, and gave me his somewhat defiant greeting. I could almost have said that he did not recognize me at the first bleared glance, and his inability, when he realized who it was, to make me feel at home, encouraged me to take the affair into my own hands.

He looked frightfully altered, but perhaps it was the shaggy beard that he had let grow over his poor, lean muzzle, that mainly made the difference. His clothes hung gauntly upon him, and he had a weak-kneed stoop. His coat sleeves were tattered at the wrists, and one of them showed the white lining at the elbow. I simply shuddered at his shirt.

"Will you smoke?" he asked huskily, almost at the first word, and with an effect of bewilderment in his hospitality that almost made me shed tears.

"Well, not just yet, Alderling," I said. "Shall I go to my old room?"

"Go anywhere," he answered, and he let me carry my bag to the chamber where I had slept before.

It was quite as his wife would have arranged it, even to the detail of a triangular portion of the bedding turned down as she used to do it for me. The place was well aired and dusted, and gave me the sense of being as immaculately clean and fresh as Alderling was not. He sat down in a chair by the window, and he remained, while I laid out my things and made my brief toilet, unabashed by those incidents for which I did not feel it necessary to banish him, if he liked staying.

We had supper by-and-by, a very well-cooked meal of fried fresh cod and potatoes, with those belated blackberries which grow so sweet when they hang long on the canes into September. There was a third plate laid, and I expected that when the housekeeper had put the dishes on the table, she would sit down with us, as the country-fashion still is, but she did not reappear till she came in with the dessert and coffee. Alderling ate hungrily, and much more than I had remembered his doing, but perhaps I formerly had the impression of Mrs. Alderling's fine appetite so strongly in mind that I had failed to note his. Certainly, however, there was a difference in one sort which I could not be mistaken in, and that was in his not talking. Her mantle of silence had fallen upon him, and whereas he used hardly to give me a chance in the conversation, he now let me do all of it. He scarcely answered my questions, and he asked none of his own; but I saw that he liked being talked to, and I did my best, shying off from his sorrow, as people foolishly do, and speaking banalities about my trip to Europe, and the Psychological Congress in Geneva, and the fellows at the club, and heaven knows what rot else.

He listened, but I do not know whether he heard much of my clack, and I got very tired of it myself at last. When I had finished my blackberries, he asked mechanically, in an echo of my former visit, with a repetition of his gesture towards the coffee-pot, "More?" I shook my head, and then he led the way out to the veranda, stopping to get his pipe and tobacco from the mantel on the way. But when we sat down in the early falling September twilight outside, he did not light his pipe, letting me smoke my cigarette alone.

"Are you off your tobacco?" I asked.

"I don't smoke," he answered, but he did not explain why, and I did not feel authorized to ask.

The talk went on as lopsidedly as before, and I began to get sleepy. I made bold to yawn, but Alderling did not mind that, and then I made bold to say that I thought I would go to bed. He followed me indoors, saying that he would go to bed, too. The hall was lighted from a hanging-lamp and two clear-burning hand-lamps which the widow had put for us on a small table. She had evidently gone home, and left us to ourselves. He took one lamp and I the other, and he started up stairs before me. If he were not coming down again, he meant to let the hanging-lamp burn, and I had nothing to say about that; but I suggested, concerning the wide-open door behind me, "Shall I close the door, Alderling?" and he answered, without looking round, "I don't shut it."

He led the way into my room, and he sat down as when I had come, and absently watched my processes of getting into bed. There was something droll, and yet miserable, in his behavior. At first, I thought he might be staying merely for the comfort of a human presence, and again, I thought he might be afraid, for I felt a little creepy myself, for no assignable reason, except that Absence, which he must have been incomparably more sensible of than I. From certain ineffectual movements that he made, and from certain preliminary noises in his throat, which ended in nothing, I decided that he wished to say something to me, tell me something, and could not. But I was selfishly sleepy, and it seemed to me that anything he had on his mind would keep there till morning, at least, and that if he got it off on mine now, it might give me a night of wakeful speculation. So when I got into bed and pulled the sheet up under my chin, I said, "Well, I don't want to turn you out, old fellow."

He stared, and answered, "Oh!" and went without other words, carrying his lamp with him and moving with a weak-kneed shuffle, like a very old man.

He was going to leave the door open behind him, but I called out, "I wish you'd shut me in, Alderling," and after a hesitation, he came back and closed the door.

VII.

We breakfasted as silently on his part as we had supped, but when we had finished, and I was wondering what he was going to let me do with myself, and on the whole what the deuce I had come for, he said, in the longest speech I had yet had from him, "Wouldn't you like to come up and see what I've been doing?"

I said I should like it immensely, and he led the way up stairs, as far As his attic studio. The door of that, like the other doors in the house, stood open, and I got the emotion which the interior gave me, full force, at the first glance. The place was so startlingly alive with that dead woman on a score of canvases in the character in which he had always painted her, that I could scarcely keep from calling out; but I went about, pretending to examine the several Madonnas, and speaking rubbish about them, while he stood stoopingly in the midst of them like the little withered old man he looked. When I had emptied myself of my chaff, I perceived that the time had come.

I glanced about for a seat, and was going to take that in which Mrs. Alderling used to pose for him, but he called out with sudden sharpness, "Not that!" and without appearing to notice, I found a box which I inverted, and sat down on.

"Tell me about your wife, Alderling," I said, and he

answered with a sort of scream, "I wanted you to ask me! Why didn't you ask me before? What did you suppose I got you here for?"

With that he shrank down, a miserable heap, in his own chair, and bowed his hapless head and cried. It was more affecting than any notion I can give you of it, and I could only wait patiently for his grief to wash itself out in one of those paroxysms which come to bereavement and leave it somehow a little comforted when they pass.

"I was waiting, for the stupid reasons you will imagine, to let you speak first," I said, "but here in her presence I couldn't hold in any longer."

He asked with strange eagerness, "You noticed that?"

I chose to feign that he meant in the pictures. "Over and over again," I answered.

He would not have my feint. "I don't mean in these wretched caricatures!"

"Well?" I assented provisionally.

"I mean her very self, listening, looking, living - waiting!"

Whether I had insanity or sorrow to deal with, I could not gainsay the unhappy man, and I only said what I really felt: "Yes, the place seems strangely full of her. I wish you would tell me about her."

He asked, with a certain slyness, "Have you heard anything about her already? At the club? From that fool woman in the kitchen?"

"For heaven's sake, no, Alderling!"

"Or about me?"

"Nothing whatever!"

He seemed relieved of whatever suspicion he felt, but he said finally, and with an air of precaution, "I should like to know just how much you mean by the place seeming full of her."

"Oh, I suppose the association of her personality with the whole house, and especially this room. I didn't mean anything preternatural, I believe."

"Then you don't believe in a life after death?" he demanded with a kind of defiance.

I thought this rather droll, seeing what his own position had been, but that was not the moment for the expression of my amusement. "The tendency is to a greater tolerance of the notion," I said. "Men like James and Royce, among the psychologists, and Shaler, among the scientists, scarcely leave us at peace in our doubts, any more, much less our denials."

He said, as if he had forgotten the question: "They called it a very light case, and they thought she was getting well. In fact, she did get well, and then - there was a relapse. They laid it to her eating some fruit which they allowed her."

Alderling spoke with a kind of bitter patience, but in my own mind I was not able to put all the blame on the doctors. Neither did I blame that innocently earthy creature, who was of no more harm in her strong appetite than any other creature which gluts its craving as simply as it feels it. The sense of her presence was deepened by the fact of those childlike self-indulgences which Alderling's words recalled to me. I made no comment, however, and he asked gloomily, as if with a return of his suspicion, "And you haven't heard of anything happening afterward?"

"I don't know what you refer to," I told him, "but I can safely say I haven't, for I haven't heard anything at all."

"They contended that it *didn't* happen," he resumed. "She died, they said, and by all the tests she had been dead two whole days. She died with her hand in mine. I was not trying to hold her back; she had a kind of majestic preoccupation in her going, so that I would not have dared to detain her if I could. You've seen them go, and how they seem to draw those last, long, deep breaths, as if they had no thought in the world but of the work of getting out of it. When her breathing stopped I expected it to go on, but it did not go on, and that was all. Nothing startling, nothing dramatic, just simple, natural, *like her!* I gave her hand back, I put it on her breast myself, and crossed the other on it. She looked as if she were sleeping, with that faint color hovering in her face, which was not wasted, but I did not make-believe about it; I accepted the fact of her death. In your 'Quests of the Occult,'" Alderling broke off, with a kind of superiority that was of almost the quality of contempt, "I believe you don't allow yourself to be daunted by a diametrical difference of opinion among the witnesses of an occurrence, as to its nature, or as to its reality, even?" "Not exactly that," I said. "I think I argued that the passive negation of one witness ought not to invalidate the testimony of another as to his experience. One might hear and see things, and strongly affirm them, and another, absorbed in something else, or in a mere suspense of the observant faculties, might quite as honestly declare that so far as his own knowledge was concerned, nothing of the kind happened. I held that in such a case, counter-testimony should not be allowed to invalidate the testimony for the fact."

"Yes, that is what I meant," said Alderling. "You say it more clearly in the book, though."

"Oh, of course."

VIII.

He began again, more remotely from the affair in hand than he had left off, as if he wanted to give himself room for parley with my possible incredulity. "You know how it was with Marion about my not believing that I should live again. Her notion was a sort of joke between us, especially when others were by, but it was a serious thing with her, in her heart. Perhaps it had originally come to her as a mere fancy, and from entertaining it playfully, she found herself with a mental inmate that finally dispossessed her judgment. You remember how literally she brought those Scripture texts to bear on it?"

"Yes. May I say that it was very affecting?"

"Affecting!" Alderling repeated in a tone of amaze at the inadequacy of my epithet. "She was always finding things that bore upon the point. After awhile she got to concealing them, as if she thought they annoyed me. They never did; they amused me; and when I saw that she had something of the sort on her mind, I would say, 'Well, out with it, Marion!' She would always begin, 'Well, you may laugh!'" and as he repeated her words Alderling did laugh, forlornly, and as I must say, rather bloodcurdlingly.

I could not prompt him to go on, but he presently did so himself, desolately enough. "I suppose, if I was in her mind at all in that supreme moment, when she seemed to be leaving this life behind with such a solemn effect of rating it at nothing, it may have been a pang to her that I was not following her into the dark, with any ray of hope for either of us. She could not have returned from it with the expectation of convincing me, for I used to tell her that if one came back from the dead, I should merely know that he had been mistaken about being dead, and was giving me a dream from his trance. She once asked me if I thought Lazarus was not really dead, with a curious childlike interest in the miracle, and she was disheartened when I reminded her that Lazarus had not testified of any life hereafter, and it did not matter whether he had been really dead or not when he was resuscitated, as far as that was concerned. Last year, we read the Bible a good deal together here, and to tease her I pretended to be convinced of the contrary by the very passages that persuaded her. As she told you, she did not care for herself. You remember that?"

"Distinctly," I said.

"It was always so. She never cared. I was perfectly aware that if she could have assured life hereafter to me, she would have given her life here to do it. You know how some women, when they are married, absolutely give themselves up, try to lose themselves in the behoof of their husbands? I don't say it rightly; there are no words that will express the utterness of their abdication."

"I know what you mean," I said, "and it was one of the facts which most interested me in Mrs. Alderling."

"Because I wasn't worthy of it? No man is!"

"It wasn't a question of that in my mind; I don't believe that occurred to me. It was the *Ding an sich* that interested me, or as it related itself to her, and not the least as it related itself to you. Such a woman's being is a cycle of self-sacrifice, so perfect, so essential, from birth to death, as to exclude the notion of volition. She is what she does. Of course she has to put her sacrifice into words from time to time, but its true language is acts, and the acts themselves only clumsily express it. There is a kind of tyranny in it for the man, of course. It requires self-sacrifice to be sacrificed to, and I don't suppose a woman has any particular merit in what is so purely natural. It appears pathetic when it is met with ingratitude or rejection, but when it has its way it is no more deserving our reverence than eating or sleeping. It astonishes men because they are as naturally incapable of it as women are capable of it."

I was mounted and was riding on, forgetful of Alderling, and what he had to tell me, if he had anything, but he recalled me to myself by having apparently forgotten me, for when I paused, he took up his affair at a quite different point, and as though that were the question in hand.

"That gift, or knack, or trick, or whatever it was, of one compelling the presence of the other by thinking or willing it, was as much mine as hers, and she tried sometimes to get me to say that I would use it with her if she died before I did; and if she were where the conditions were opposed to her coming to me, my will would help her to overcome the hinderance; our united wills would form a current of volition that she could travel back on against all obstacles. I don't know whether I make myself clear?" he appealed.

"Yes, perfectly," I said. "It is very curious." He said in a kind of muse, "I don't know just where I was." Then he began again, "Oh, yes! It was at the ceremony - down there in the library. Some of the country people came in; I suppose they thought they ought, and I suppose they wanted to; it didn't matter to me. I had sent for Doctor Norrey, as soon as the relapse came, and he was there with me. Of course there was the minister, conducting the services. He made a prayer full of helpless repetitions, which I helplessly noticed, and some scrambling remarks, mostly misdirected at me, affirming and reaffirming that the sister they had lost was only gone before, and that she was now in a happier world.

"The singing and the praying and the preaching came to an end, and then there was that soul-sickening hush, that exanimate silence, of which the noise of rustling clothes and scraping feet formed a part, as the people rose in the hall, where chairs had been put for them, leaving me and Norrey alone with Marion. Every fibre of my frame recognized the moment of parting, and protested. A tremendous wave of will swept through me and from me, a resistless demand for her presence, and it had power upon her. I heard her speak, and say, as distinctly as I repeat the words, 'I will come for you!' and the youth and the beauty that had been growing more and more wonderful in her face, ever since she died, shone like a kind of light from it. I answered her, 'I am ready now!' and then Norrey scuffled to his feet, with a conventional face of sympathy, and said, 'No hurry, my dear Alderling,' and I knew he had not heard or seen anything, as well as I did afterwards when I questioned him. He thought I was giving them notice that they could take her away. What do you think?"

"How what do I think?" I asked.

"Do you think that it happened?"

There was something in Alderling's tone and manner that made me, instead of answering directly that I did not, temporize and ask, "Why?"

"Because - because," and Alderling caught his breath, like a child that is trying to keep itself from crying, "because *I* don't." He broke into a sobbing that seemed to wrench and tear his poor little body, and if I had thought of anything to say, I could not have said it to his headlong grief with any hope of assuaging it. "I am satisfied now," he said, at last, wiping his wet face, and striving for some composure of its trembling features, "that it was all a delusion, the effect of my exaltation, of my momentary aberration, perhaps. Don't be afraid of saying what you really think," he added scornfully, "with the notion of sparing me. You couldn't doubt it, or deny it, more completely than I do."

I confess this unexpected turn struck me dumb. I did not try to say anything, and Alderling went on.

"I don't deny that she is living, but I can't believe that I shall ever live to see her again, or if you prefer, die to see her. There is the play of the poor animal instinct, or the mechanical persistence of expectation in me, so that I can't shut the doors without the sense of shutting her out, can't put out the lights without feeling that I am leaving her in the dark. But I know it is all foolishness, as well as you do, all craziness. If she is alive it is because she believed she should live, and I shall perish because I didn't believe. I should like to believe, now, if only to see her again, but it is too late. If you disuse any member of your body, or any faculty of your mind, it withers away and if you deny your soul your soul ceases to be."

I found myself saying, "That is very interesting," from a certain force of habit, which you have noted in me, when confronted with a novel instance of any kind. "But," I suggested, "why not act upon the reverse of that principle, and create the fact by affirmation which you think your denial destroys?"

"Because," he repeated wearily, "it is too late. You might as well ask the fakir who has held his arm upright for twenty years, till it has stiffened there, to restore the dry stock by exercise. It is too late, I tell you."

"But, look here, Alderling," I pursued, beginning to taste the joy of argument. "You say that your will had such power upon her after you knew her to be dead that you made her speak to you?"

"No, I don't say that now," he returned. "I know now that it was a delusion."

"But if you once had that power of summoning her to you, by strongly wishing for her presence, when you were both living here, why doesn't it stand to reason that you could do it still, if she is living there and you are living here?"

"I never had any such power," he replied, with the calm of absolute tragedy. "That was a delusion too. I leave the doors open for her, night and day, because I must, but if she came I should know it was not she."

IX.

Of course you know your own business, my dear Acton, but if you think of using the story of the Alderlings - and there is no reason why you should not, for they are both dead, without kith or kin surviving, so far as I know, unless he has some relatives in Germany, who would never penetrate the disguise you could give the case - it seems to me that here is your true climax. But I necessarily leave the matter to you, for I shall not touch it at any point where we could come into competition. In fact, I doubt if I ever touch it at all, for though all psychology is in a manner dealing with the occult, still I think I have done my duty by that side of it, as the occult is usually understood; and I am shy of its grosser instances, as things that are apt to bring one's scientific poise into question. However, you shall be the judge of what is best for you to do, when you have the whole story, and I will give it you without more ado, merely premising that I have a sort of shame for the aptness of the catastrophe. I shall respect you more if I hear that you agree with me as to the true climax of the tragedy, and have the heroism to reject the final event.

I stayed with Alderling nearly a week, and I will own that I bored myself. In fact, I am not sure but we bored each other. At any rate, when I told him, the night before I intended going, that I meant to leave him in the morning, he seemed resigned, or indifferent, or perhaps merely inattentive. From time to time we had recurred to the matter of his experience, or his delusion, but with apparently increasing impatience on his part, and certainly decreasing interest on mine; so that at last I think he was willing to have me go. But in the morning he seemed reluctant, and pleaded with me to stay a few days longer with him. I alleged engagements, more or less unreal, for I was never on such terms with Alderling that I felt I need make any special sacrifice to him. He gave way, suspiciously, rather, and when I came down from my room after having put the last touches to my packing, I found him on the veranda looking out to seaward, where a heavy fog-bank hung.

You will sense here the sort of *patness* which I feel cheapens the catastrophe; and yet, as I consider it, again, the fact is not without its curious importance, and its bearing upon what went before. I do not know but it gives the whole affair a relief which it would not otherwise have.

He was to have driven me to the station, some miles away, before noon, and I supposed we should sit down together, and try to have some sort of talk before I went. But Alderling appeared to have forgotten about my going, and after a while, took himself off to his studio, and left me alone to watch the inroads of the fog. It came on over the harbor rapidly, as on that morning when Mrs. Alderling had been so nearly lost in it, and presently the masts and shrouds of the shipping at anchor were sticking up out of it as if they were sunk into a body as dense as the sea under them.

I amused myself watching it blot out one detail of the prospect after another, while the fog-horn lowed through it, and the bell-buoy, far out beyond the light-house ledge, tolled mournfully. The milk-white mass moved landward,

WILLIAM DEAN HOWELLS

and soon the air was blind with the mist which hid the grass twenty yards away. There was an awfulness in the silence, which nothing broke but the lowing of the horn, and the tolling of the bell, except when now and then the voice of a sailor came through it, like that of some drowned man sending up his hail from the bottom of the bay.

Suddenly I heard a joyful shout from the attic overhead:

"I am coming! I am coming!"

It was Alderling calling out through his window, and then a cry came from over the water, which seemed to answer him, but which there is no reason in the world to believe was not a girlish shout from one of the yachts, swallowed up in the fog.

His lunging descent of the successive stairways followed, and he burst through the doorway beside me, and without heeding me, ran bareheaded down the sloping lawn.

I followed, with what notion of help or hinderance I should not find it easy to say, but before I reached the water's edge - in fact I never did reach it, and had some difficulty making my way back to the house, - I heard the rapid throb of the oars in the row-locks as he pulled through the white opacity.

You know the rest, for it was the common property of our enterprising press at the time, when the incident was fully reported, with my ineffectual efforts to be satisfactorily interviewed as to the nothing I knew.

The oarless boat was found floating far out to sea after the fog lifted. It was useless to look for Alderling's body, and I do not know that any search was made for it.

Choose from Thousands of 1stWorldLibrary Classics By

Adolphus WilliamWard
Aesop
Agatha Christie
Alexander Aaronsohn
Alexander Kielland
Alexandre Dumas
Alfred Gatty
Alfred Ollivant
Alice Duer Miller
Alice Turner Curtis
Alice Dunbar
Ambrose Bierce
Amelia E. Barr
Andrew Lang
Andrew McFarland Davis
Anna Sewell
Annie Besant
Annie Hamilton Donnell
Annie Payson Call
Anton Chekhov
Arnold Bennett
Arthur Conan Doyle
Arthur Ransome
Atticus
B. M. Bower
Basil King
Bayard Taylor
Ben Macomber
Booth Tarkington
Bram Stoker
C. Collodi
C. E. Orr
C. M. Ingleby
Carolyn Wells
Catherine Parr Traill
Charles A. Eastman
Charles Dickens
Charles Dudley Warner
Charles Farrar Browne
Charles Ives
Charles Kingsley
Charles Lathrop Pack
Charles Whibley
Charles Willing Beale
Charlotte M. Braeme
Charlotte M.Yonge
Clair W. Hayes
Clarence Day Jr.
Clarence E. Mulford

Clemence Housman
Confucius
Cornelis DeWitt Wilcox
Cyril Burleigh
D. H. Lawrence
Daniel Defoe
David Garnett
Don Carlos Janes
Donald Keyhole
Dorothy Kilner
Dougan Clark
E. Nesbit
E.P.Roe
E. Phillips Oppenheim
Edgar Allan Poe
Edgar Rice Burroughs
Edith Wharton
Edward J. O'Biren
John Cournos
Edwin L. Arnold
Eleanor Atkins
Elizabeth Cleghorn
Gaskell
Elizabeth Von Arnim
Ellem Key
Emily Dickinson
Erasmus W. Jones
Ernie Howard Pie
Ethel Turner
Ethel Watts Mumford
Eugenie Foa
Eugene Wood
Evelyn Everett-Green
Everard Cotes
F. J. Cross
Federick Austin Ogg
Ferdinand Ossendowski
Francis Bacon
Francis Darwin
Frances Hodgson Burnett
Frank Gee Patchin
Frank Harris
Frank Jewett Mather
Frank L. Packard
Frederick Trevor Hill
Frederick Winslow Taylor
Friedrich Kerst
Friedrich Nietzsche
Fyodor Dostoyevsky

Gabrielle E. Jackson
Garrett P. Serviss
Gaston Leroux
George Ade
Geroge Bernard Shaw
George Ebers
George Eliot
George MacDonald
George Orwell
George Tucker
George W. Cable
George Wharton James
Gertrude Atherton
Grace E. King
Grant Allen
Guillermo A. Sherwell
Gulielma Zollinger
Gustav Flaubert
H. A. Cody
H. B. Irving
H. G. Wells
H. H. Munro
H. Irving Hancock
H. Rider Haggard
H. W. C. Davis
Hamilton Wright Mabie
Hans Christian Andersen
Harold Avery
Harold McGrath
Harriet Beecher Stowe
Harry Houidini
Helent Hunt Jackson
Helen Nicolay
Hendy David Thoreau
Henrik Ibsen
Henry Adams
Henry Ford
Henry Frost
Henry James
Henry Jones Ford
Henry Seton Merriman
Henry Wadsworth
Longfellow
Henry W Longfellow
Herbert A. Giles
Herbert N. Casson
Herman Hesse
Homer
Honore De Balzac

Horace Walpole
Horatio Alger, Jr.
Howard Pyle
Howard R. Garis
Hugh Lofting
Hugh Walpole
Humphry Ward
Ian Maclaren
Israel Abrahams
J.G.Austin
J. Henri Fabre
J. M. Barrie
J. Macdonald Oxley
J. S. Knowles
J. Storer Clouston
Jack London
Jacob Abbott
James Allen
James Lane Allen
James Andrews
James Baldwin
James DeMille
James Joyce
James Oliver Curwood
James Oppenheim
James Otis
Jane Austen
Jens Peter Jacobsen
Jerome K. Jerome
John Burroughs
John F. Kennedy
John Gay
John Glasworthy
John Habberton
John Joy Bell
John Milton
John Philip Sousa
Jonathan Swift
Joseph Carey
Joseph Conrad
Joseph Jacobs
Julian Hawthrone
Julies Vernes
Justin Huntly McCarthy
Kakuzo Okakura
Kenneth Grahame
Kate Langley Bosher
L. A. Abbot
L. T. Meade
L. Frank Baum
Laura Lee Hope

Laurence Housman
Leo Tolstoy
Leonid Andreyev
Lewis Carroll
Lilian Bell
Lloyd Osbourne
Louis Tracy
Louisa May Alcott
Lucy Fitch Perkins
Lucy Maud Montgomery
Lydia Miller Middleton
Lyndon Orr
M. H. Adams
Margaret E. Sangster
Margaret Vandercook
Maria Edgeworth
Maria Thompson Daviess
Mariano Azuela
Marion Polk Angellotti
Mark Overton
Mark Twain
Mary Austin
Mary Cole
Mary Rowlandson
Mary Wollstonecraft
Shelley
Max Beerbohm
Myra Kelly
Nathaniel Hawthrone
O. F. Walton
Oscar Wilde
Owen Johnson
P.G.Wodehouse
Paul and Mable Thorn
Paul G. Tomlinson
Paul Severing
Peter B. Kyne
Plato
R. Derby Holmes
R. L. Stevenson
Rabindranath Tagore
Rahul Alvares
Ralph Waldo Emmerson
Rene Descartes
Rex E. Beach
Richard Harding Davis
Richard Jefferies
Robert Barr
Robert Frost
Robert Gordon Anderson
Robert L. Drake

Robert Lansing
Robert Michael Ballantyne
Robert W. Chambers
Rosa Nouchette Carey
Ross Kay
Rudyard Kipling
Samuel B. Allison
Samuel Hopkins Adams
Sarah Bernhardt
Selma Lagerlof
Sherwood Anderson
Sigmund Freud
Standish O'Grady
Stanley Weyman
Stella Benson
Stephen Crane
Stewart Edward White
Stijn Streuvels
Swami Abhedananda
Swami Parmananda
T. S. Ackland
The Princess Der Ling
Thomas A. Janvier
Thomas A Kempis
Thomas Anderton
Thomas Bailey Aldrich
Thomas Bulfinch
Thomas De Quincey
Thomas H. Huxley
Thomas Hardy
Thomas More
Thornton W. Burgess
U. S. Grant
Valentine Williams
Victor Appleton
Virginia Woolf
Walter Scott
Washington Irving
Wilbur Lawton
Wilkie Collins
Willa Cather
Willard F. Baker
William Makepeace
Thackeray
William W. Walter
Winston Churchill
Yei Theodora Ozaki
Young E. Allison
Zane Grey

www.ingramcontent.com/pod-product-compliance
Lightning Source LLC
Chambersburg PA
CBHW051827170626
46807CB00003B/1061